CAUGHT IN TRAFFIC
The Sydney Roberts Series–Book Two

Susan Hart Snyder

Cover Design by Micah Kearns
Author Photo by Patti Sewall

Caught in Traffic/Susan Hart Snyder -- 2nd Ed.
ISBN-13: 978-0-9974224-2-9
LCCN: 2015908175

To my editor Christmas Cowell, who stands as testimony to the ability of the human spirit to approach both life's adversities and its blessings with a generous attitude and cheerful heart.
It is a privilege to call her *friend*.

A journey is a person in itself; no two are alike. And all plans, safeguards, policing, and coercion are fruitless. We find that after years of struggle that we do not take a trip; a trip takes us.

John Steinbeck

CHAPTER ONE

Feet. Becoming a world-renowned expert on them was not exactly what I had in mind when I decided to move to New York. But, an expert I am, due to all the time I spent staring up at them through the two transom windows in my cousin Ralph's basement apartment in the Bronx.

Ever on the lookout for excuses to tear myself away from my actual work, I made a study of concocting an entire life from the bottom twelve inches of a person's attire.

For instance, practical shoes with well-worn soles, stockings bunched around the ankles, and a slow but steady pace designate a lonely widow. Her most exciting event of the day is venturing outside to empty her wastebasket of its meager contents. White socks with black loafers define a widower with the same bio.

That actual work I was so good at avoiding was copy editing for one of New York's large publishing houses. It was a step down from the editing work I had done in L.A., but I took it because it paid the bills. One of the perks was I could work at home, only having to go into Manhattan twice a week. It was definitely a time and money saver since Ralph's place was on the north side of the Bronx.

Ralph told me the commute was the trade-off for putting a whole lot of numbered streets between us and areas to the south that were a far cry from my L.A. neighborhood. I took his word for it.

It was tough giving up the familiarity of L.A., but at thirty-three, it was more than time. I had lived in Southern California all my life, and was in a relationship that, after five years, felt like it was never going to get off the couch. Add to that my nagging belief that a life should matter, and the harsh reality that mine didn't, made me ripe for a move, both physical and mental.

Ralph's area was a quiet place of modest houses and apartments, and great parks. The inhabitants, although not nearly as perky as Southern Californians, seemed approachable.

The parks were a bonus, as Mr. Bumbles, my Basset Hound, was a whole lot happier sniffing and piddling on the requisite two-dozen bushes a day. Alice, my black and white cat, took the opposite view, preferring to do her business in the comfort of her own home. It was just as well. I was uneasy about letting her outside. I was pretty sure no one would steal her. Her orneriness was a definite deterrent. But I didn't want to risk her running away or getting hit by a car.

Mr. Bumbles' piddle walks usually took place midmorning and midafternoon. They were our reward for my completing a pre-determined amount of editing. It was important for my mental health to expand my sphere beyond feet.

Stepping away from my desk, I was more than ready for my afternoon jaunt with Mr. Bumbles. As I started to grab his leash I noticed the pair of feet that appeared in my transom window almost every day. They were outfitted in sports shoes that intrigued me because they looked like they were made of cork, and were trimmed in red leather. I imagined their owner was a spoiled teenage boy with little ambition and no clue about the cost of his shoes relative to the salary of the worker who made them.

My opinion may have been clouded by my run-in with delinquent taggers in a small town in Harmony, Utah, where I broke down on my way to New York. They had made a mess of the motorhome I was driving, my part of a trade with Ralph for a few months in his basement. Ralph was none too happy when he took a gander at the mottled body of the RV. It was an abstract of green and pink spray-painted obscenities thinly covered with white paint that I hired another teenager to apply.

Fortunately, as the manager of an auto parts store in Yonkers, Ralph had a buddy with an auto body shop. He had the equipment to do a whole lot better job covering the graffiti. I was paying Ralph back for delivering blemished goods in ale from the local pub.

What differentiated those cork-covered feet was they generally stopped at the far edge of Ralph's lot line, and were met by another pair of feet that were rarely the same two days in a row. I was curious enough about Cork Feet guy that I poked my head out of my hovel on a couple of occasions, but the feet and everything above them were gone by the time I got up there.

After hooking Mr. Bumbles' leash to his collar, I noticed Cork Feet was still there, so I hurried to see if I could catch a look. When Mr. B and I walked out the door, I witnessed the tail end of an exchange that looked a lot like a drug deal. Or, was that just my suspicious nature flaring up?

Not wanting to draw their attention, I occupied myself with adjusting Mr. B's collar, but kept my eyes on Cork Feet as he hurried away. An oversized blue baseball cap covered his head, and his hair stuck out from under it like long brown straw. I guessed that he was about fifteen. As I straightened up, the other young man strode past me, also in a rush. He looked to be about five years older and was wearing a similar oversized blue baseball cap.

Since Cork Feet was heading in the direction of the park, I decided to follow him. I don't know what I expected to find, but it had the potential to be a lot more stimulating than the romance novels I was editing, those of the bursting bodices and throbbing loins. It was truly amazing how a writer could manage to make sex a yawner. After editing several of them, all I could think was, enough already, just get on with it and spare us the agonizing detail, or let the king's men lock the bloody bastard in the dungeon and throw away the dang key!

I'm not much of a romantic, I guess.

I only caught a glimpse of the blue baseball cap before it disappeared around a corner, with Mr. B unwilling to be sidetracked from his sniffathon. When we arrived at the park, we wove our way into the heart of it, passing a group of girls kicking soccer balls back and forth, their thick ponytails swinging in time with their footwork.

Stopping for the umpteenth time for Mr. B to pee, I inhaled and breathed in the first crisp hint of autumn. Or, at least that's what I thought it was. As a native Southern Californian, I was unfamiliar with that particular season, at least in the traditional form. For us, fall was brush fires and Santa Ana winds. Here, the promise of fire was in the scarlet hues of the leaves and the warmth of brick hearths.

I turned my neck from side to side to work out the kinks that are one of the main hazards of a profession that is also known to cause broad butt disease. Catching a glimpse of a blue baseball cap off in the distance, I decided to investigate. When I was near enough to make out the red trim on his shoes, I knew I had found Cork Feet. He was sitting on top of a picnic table, his feet resting on the bench.

Using the trees as a shield, I moved closer. Sitting on the bench below him was an older man dressed in a soiled canvas jacket and worn black twill pants. At the man's feet was a large overstuffed duffle with a broken zipper. He was faced away from Cork Feet, his arms resting on his legs, his gaze focused on the ground. They were engaged in a conversation of few words, with long pauses interrupted by slight movement when one or the other of them spoke.

With little to hold my interest, I decided I had done enough spying for the day and turned to walk Mr. B back to the basement. Catching movement from the picnic table out of the corner of my eye, I looked over to see Cork Feet hold out his fist and pass something to the man, who reached down to stuff what he had been handed into the bottom of the duffle.

Hmm. Cork Feet had to be dealing. I decided to run my theory by Ralph to see if illicit drugs were a problem in the neighborhood.

After dropping Mr. Bumbles off in the basement, I took the stairs up to Ralph's, knocking on the door that separated it from the entry. Although he said to come in anytime, I didn't feel like we knew each other well enough for an open door policy. Even though our fathers had been brothers who talked quite often, the two of us had only seen each other twice while growing up. Once when Ralph and his brother Tom had hounded their parents enough to be taken to Disneyland. The other when my mother, father and I made our obligatory pilgrimage to ancestral sites in New York, with a side trip to the Statue of Liberty.

Ralph and I became reacquainted when he flew out to L.A. to attend the memorial service for our Uncle George, the oldest of the three brothers. My father Daniel and he had hitchhiked out to L.A. to find work when they were in their early twenties, while Ralph's father Norman, the youngest, stayed behind. It seemed strange they were all gone. Damn. I didn't like it. I really missed my dad–and mom.

Uncle George had never married. That's how I ended up with the motorhome I traded to Ralph. I held onto the Sandy Koufax bobblehead doll and Dodger cap that came with it, although I planned on keeping my allegiance to the Dodgers to myself. I was highly aware that I had landed deep in Yankee territory, and I didn't think I was quite gutsy enough to take on Bronx Bomber fans.

When I didn't hear any footsteps heading to the door, I looked at my watch. It was about the time Ralph usually came home from work, so I knocked again. When the door finally opened, it wasn't him. It was a little lady with the biggest, brightest hair I had ever seen on someone her size and age. Now, I have enough red hair to be the subject of discussion more often than I would like, but hers? It was a color totally unknown to nature; a mixture of magenta and burnished orange that looked like it had been whipped up in a blender. Wow!

Dragging my eyes away from her hair to her face, recognition dawned. It was my Aunt Felicia, Ralph's mother. It was the first time I had seen her since I arrived in New York, and she didn't look like my memory of her at all. The Aunt Felicia I knew was a gray-haired, pinch-faced mouse. The woman standing in front of me–well, I don't know exactly what she was going for–but, she was far more cat than mouse.

Especially with those bright, gold high-heeled sandals, I marveled, looking at her feet. They weren't ones I had seen from my transom windows, but definitely created their own story of a widow who wasn't about to settle for the highlight of her day being a trip to the dumpster. No. Aunt Felicia's life had clearly become more colorful since the death of Uncle Norman. *Clearly.* I concentrated on not gawking at her hair.

"Oh, hi, Aunt Felicia." I wasn't sure whether to stick out my hand or go in for a hug.

Narrowing her tweezed brows, she looked up at me, suspicion moving across her eyes. She didn't respond.

"It's Sydney, you know, Daniel's daughter." I held out my hand, definitely the better choice.

"Sydney." She allowed me to wrap my long fingers around her small bony ones. "I would have never recognized you, darling. You're so tall, and all that red hair, my word."

"I've always had the red hair, you may recall." Of course we ended up talking about *my* hair.

"Yes. But, there's so much of it. Is it a wig?" She moved her head around as if trying to get a better look.

"No. It's all mine." To prove it, I tugged on a lock.

"Do you dye it yourself, or does someone else do it?"

"Neither. Like I said, it's all mine."

"Well, it's a great color, darling." She tapped her upper lip with the long tapering bright red nail of her index finger. "I'd like to have Ralph's girlfriend Penny take a look at it, you know, see if she can match it for me." Studying my head as if it was an endangered species, she stepped into the entryway and around behind me.

Okay, enough with the hair. Aren't you even curious about why I'm standing at Ralph's doorstep, or what I've been doing for the last twenty years? I turned so I was facing her again. "Did Ralph tell you I ..."

"You know, this is a wig, darling," she interrupted, as if she hadn't heard me, and patted her hair.

"I never would have guessed," I said, with just enough sarcasm that her eyes questioned my intent. I quickly covered with, "It's truly amazing."

Satisfied, she continued, "So anyway, darling, Penny orders them for me, dyes and styles them. She's a miracle worker, honestly. I know she'd be able to do something with that cut of yours."

"Oh." I reached up to pat my own hair. I didn't think there was anything wrong with my cut. It was getting a little poufy since my last appointment with my L.A. hairdresser, but I didn't think it was *that* bad.

"Ask Ralph to introduce you to Penny. See if she has any openings."

Maybe it *was* that bad. And this coming from a woman whose wig could be stuck on the end of a paper cone and sold as cotton candy. "I've actually met Penny. Didn't Ralph tell you I moved into the basement apartment?" I gestured to the staircase.

"No." She wrapped her scarlet-tipped fingers around her waist. "I haven't heard from my son in weeks. Are you paying him rent?"

Whoa, I didn't see that one coming. I suddenly felt like I was on trial. "Um, well," I stammered, while deciding whether Ralph's and my arrangement was any of her business.

"You know, I own the second on this thing, darling." She lifted her chin to the front door in a proprietary gesture.

"No, I didn't know that."

"My son's idea. 'Ma,' he says, 'I take out a second with you, and you earn the interest instead of the bank. You'll make way more than with a savings account.' So, I loan him the money, and what? I may as well have stuffed it under my mattress for all the interest I've made."

Okay. How was I supposed to respond to that? Not a worry as it turns out, because she was just warming up.

"Every month it's the same thing. I wait, and does he bring me my payment, or even mail it to me? Never. And, it's not like I'm flush with cash. I need that money. I have expenses."

Right. I watched her wig bob up and down with her annoyance. Those things can't be cheap.

"So here I am, once again having to come to him, like some beggar on the street. I don't know how a boy can do that to his own mother. Have you seen him? He has to be here. His car is parked down the street."

"No, I haven't. Wouldn't you rather go inside and wait for him there." I nodded toward the door, hoping my suggestion would allow me to disappear into my basement and leave Ralph and his mother to work out their issues without me. I didn't know why she felt compelled to share, maybe because we were related, or more likely because she shared with anyone with an ear.

"I don't have any more time for this." She looked at her watch and squeezed her lined lips together. "My mahjong group is coming over tonight, and I have to get ready. Wait here while I get my purse, and walk me to my car. I don't like to be on this street after dark."

Looking through the entry sidelight, it didn't appear to be dark, more just the tail end of afternoon, but I said, "Okay." I wasn't going to argue with her.

Escorting Aunt Felicia up the street, I wondered how she managed to stay upright on her high heels, but she just clipped along. Being that short, maybe she had a lot of practice. At five feet eleven, you'd never find *me* in shoes that high. The ground is far enough away as it is.

Stopping beside a very long nineties mauve Cadillac, she pulled her purse from her arm and dug for her keys. How on earth did she park, let alone drive the thing? From the dents on the side panels and bumpers, the answer was, not that well.

"I see you noticed my dents. It's embarrassing!" She caught me looking at them.

"They're not that bad." I tried to downplay her discomfort at her obvious lack of skill behind the wheel.

"Here, my son is in the automobile business. I've been asking him to do something about these for months." She pointed at the car. "And, has he? Of course not." Apparently, it was Ralph who was supposed to be embarrassed. She wasn't about to take any responsibility for driving like a demolition derby contestant.

Not wanting to touch on that topic either, I kept quiet, crossed my arms, and looked up the block while she went back to fumbling for her keys. There were a lot of people out on the street, with a little more pep in their step because it was Friday. I loved that about New York. Not having to rely on crowded freeways to commute was heaven. And, with the virtuosity of the added exercise, I got to order dessert without a side of guilt. Yay.

Among the walkers making their way toward us I spotted Ralph sauntering along with a brown paper sack cradled under his arm. He started to wave when he saw me, but immediately dropped his hand when he noticed his mother. Ducking down, he scurried between two compact cars parked at the curb.

Coward.

The top of his balding head was still visible, which he must have figured out, because it inched toward the street and then disappeared.

I looked back over at Aunt Felicia, who had found her keys and was rounding the back of her car to the driver's side. "You tell that son of mine to call me." She set her purse on the trunk. "Preferably sometime before I take my last breath."

"Okay." Trying to keep one eye on the last place I saw Ralph, I wondered whether to shout, *There he is!* or to play along with this juvenile game of his. Jeez. It was Ralph's problem, and here I was feeling like I was about to get caught and sent to the principal's office.

"And, take my advice on calling Penny now, darling." She zipped her purse shut. "Again, a miracle worker, I'm telling you."

"Okay. Nice seeing you," I said as she disappeared behind the sedan, hoping she was not the type who fiddled forever before starting a car. This was way too much tension for me.

Sensing movement from up the street, I saw Ralph peek out from behind a small SUV, two cars beyond the compact. When he didn't see his mother, he turned his hands up as if to ask me if it was safe to come out. I held my palm out to stop him, gesturing for him to stay low, then gave him the all clear when she pulled away from the curb.

Did the guy have no shame? More than one of the passersby on the street had stared over at him like he was either dangerous, nuts, or both.

He didn't seem to mind. When he finally reappeared, his brown bag tucked back under his arm, he was once again in sauntering mode.

"Hey, cuz." He stepped up beside me.

"Hey, Ralph."

"Beer!" He shifted the bag from under his arm and patted it. "Penny and her friends are coming over. You want to come up?"

So, nothing about your having spent the last five minutes crouched behind a car? "Your mother says to call her." I was a little too much of a goody two shoes to let the whole incident slide by without comment, a trait that generally took me to places I later regretted going.

"Yeah, yeah, I'll get to it."

I cocked my head, debating whether I wanted to dig into the problems between a thirty-five-year-old man and his mother. Nope. Not at all. "A beer sounds great. What time?"

CHAPTER TWO

Sitting at Ralph's kitchen table, he had just handed a beer to me when a cacophony of high voices bounced down the hallway. It was his girlfriend, Penny, and two friends dressed in short stretchy skirts and attitude.

Penny crossed the room, her breasts squeezed above a deep v-cut orange top that was even tighter than her skirt. "Hi, baby." She slid her arm around Ralph, kissed him on the cheek and moved past him to the refrigerator. Opening it, she pulled out a beer in one hand and a bottle of white wine in the other, and held them out to her friends. "Which?"

"Wine," they said in unison.

"Ralphy, get some glasses, would ya?" Penny grabbed an opener from a drawer, and took it and the wine to the table. "Sit, sit," she said to her friends. "This is Ralph's cousin, Sydney." She pointed her chin at me as she opened the wine. "Sydney, this is Courtney." She moved her chin in the direction of the friend with blue-black hair layered around her face and halfway down her back, and a body she had molded to snap necks. She slid into the seat across from mine.

"And that's Leeza." Penny set the opener down and nodded at the friend with closely cropped platinum-blonde hair and large blue eyes accentuated by jet black liner she had tapered up and out from her lids in cat-eye fashion. She sat down next to me.

"Sydney's living in Ralph's basement." Penny filled the glasses, as Ralph scooted a chair across the linoleum floor to the table and set it beside her.

"My condolences," Courtney said in a high-pitched nasally tone. "I hope you had it fumigated."

"Yeah, that man cave was disgusting," Leeza joined in.

"Hey, I cleaned it up." Ralph had turned his chair around and was straddling it, his wrists resting on the top rail, a beer in one hand.

"You and what army?" Courtney laughed. "Did he clear a path for you through the empty bottles, Sydney?" she asked, pronouncing my name as *Syd-a-ney*. That was a new one.

"I hauled them away. Not a bottle left, right, Syd?" Ralph took a swig of his beer.

Before I could reply to the state of the basement, Leeza said, "Oh good, you hear that, Penny? He probably scored enough recycle cash to take you to the Bahamas. Start packing." She held up her glass in a mock toast.

"Yeah, maybe while you're down there, you can scout out a place for a wedding. What do ya say, Ralphy?" Courtney reached for her wine. "You gonna give us the pleasure of a destination wedding in the Caribbean?"

"You two are engaged?" I spoke up.

"I don't know," Penny answered. "Are we, Ralphy?" Her tone was sweet, but her smile was as mocking as Leeza's toast.

Ralph shifted in his seat. "Hey, I'm outnumbered here. Take it easy on me." He quickly changed the subject. "We're heading to Bridie O'Brien's, at about what, eight? Andy and Jared want to meet us there." Setting his beer down, he pulled his cellphone out of his pocket, not waiting for an answer. "I'll let 'em know."

Courtney and Leeza rolled their eyes and looked over at Penny. Penny shrugged her shoulders, sighing at the thinning brown hair of Ralph's head bent over his phone.

Okay, I was really sorry I asked the question. This was clearly a subject with a history, and as with Ralph's mother, I didn't want to have anything to do with it.

"You coming along to the pub?" Penny turned her eyes from Ralph to me.

"I don't know." I searched my brain for a polite out, while thinking I didn't exactly fit in with Ralph's group of friends. It was funny that I felt more at home with the country folks I met in Harmony, Utah than I did with these New Yorkers. And I was a city girl too. It could also have to do with my longing for Noah, a good-looking cowboy, who I became a tad more familiar with than the others. He hadn't been off my mind a single day since I left Harmony.

"It doesn't sound like you've been getting out of the basement much, Sydney, does it Ralphy?" Penny looked at me, then over to him.

"Huh?" He glanced up after she called his name a second time. "What?"

"Sydney. Didn't you say that Sydney was spending all her time in the basement?"

"Yeah, yeah."

"We want her to come along to Bridie's."

"Sure, you should come." He looked over at me, then back at the phone. A man of few words.

"You *have to* come," Courtney added in her whiny tone that was already starting to grate on me. Her voice was not her best asset. But then again, most guys were probably more focused on things south of her mouth.

"Yeah, it's Malachi night." Leeza crossed her legs and turned toward me. "You want to be there, I promise."

"Malachi night?" I said.

"Yeah. Malachi Keane is performing." Leeza pretended to fan her face. "Oh my God. He's *so hot*."

"That Irish accent," Courtney added. "I'd like to be the pot of gold at the end of *his* rainbow." She let out a sharp honking laugh at her own joke, which made me jump. Maybe she had a deviated septum.

"You're not doing anything else, are you?" Penny asked.

"Well no, not really." I was unable to produce a plausible excuse.

"Good, then it's settled. You're coming." She took a sip of her wine then set the glass on the table. "There's plenty of time for you to change."

Looking down at my sweater and jeans, I wondered why they weren't acceptable for the pub. I had worn them there before.

Penny noticed my hesitation. "It's Friday night. There'll be lots of single guys there. Time to get your sexy on, woman. Who knows, with all that red hair, Malachi might think you're Irish."

My sexy on, huh? If she thought we were going to become a quartet of spandex skirts, she was going to be disappointed, Malachi or not. There was no rubberized clothing in my life now, and none planned for the future. I appreciated Penny's good intentions regarding my social life. She seemed like a nice person, but really, did she have to comment on my hair like everyone else? As a hairdresser, I suppose she was about the only one who had license to say something. I thought perhaps I ought to set my ego aside and see if she could come up with a style that would make the red less of a fascination for people. "Ralph's mother thinks you're a miracle worker with hair. I haven't had a chance to get mine done since I left L.A."

"I'd love to work on it. I'm a master at cuts and blowouts. I'll help you with your skin too, if you like."

Blowouts? Do something about my skin? So much for setting my ego aside. Maybe I should have just stayed in my basement.

I must have reddened from embarrassment, because she said, "Some of my clients would spend big bucks for hair your color. You know, red is really hard to get right."

"So, I've heard." Like about a thousand times.

"I'm sure I'll be able to work you in some time next week."

"Thanks." After that exchange, I was even less convinced I wanted to spend the evening with them. "I should get changed," I added, knowing I would go anyway.

"Fun tonight." Penny poured more wine for Courtney and Leeza. All three lifted their glasses. "Party, party!" They clicked them together in what appeared to be a ritual they had performed many times before.

Ralph was still buried in his texting. Were he my boyfriend-slash-fiancé, I would have ripped the cellphone out of his hands. But, I had a feeling my cousin was the secondary plot to the adventures of the three women who were now gyrating around the room.

When we walked into Bridie O'Brien's, it was already pulsing with warm bodies seeking to tear down the personal space boundaries that had walled them in all week. Funny how thigh to thigh contact in a bar was a whole lot more welcome than the same contact in a subway car.

The bar was one of those warm wood-paneled places reminiscent of pubs all over the world that make everyone want to be Irish, at least for the night. The bartenders knew how to pour a proper glass of Guinness, something I was told on my first visit is an inviolate rule for an establishment of that type.

I snaked my way around the bar and through the crowd, following the exaggerated hip undulations of Penny and her friends, to a table by a small stage. I personally kept my own undulating to a minimum, still somewhat incredulous at the bigger-the-better butt trend. Waiting for us at the table were Ralph's friends, Andy and Jared. I had met them before, and they were nice enough guys, but it was obvious why they were all friends. They were the Lost Boys to Ralph's Peter Pan.

Having picked up on Andy's interest in me during our last time together, I purposely grabbed a chair across the table from him. No sense in encouraging something that was never going to happen. My aim for my move was to step out of my comfort zone, and to fill that gnawing void where purpose was supposed to reside. I watched Andy flip the bill of his baseball cap to the back of his head after taking a long swig of his dark beer. With him, I would clearly not be making forward progress.

I also gave up a one-week relationship in Harmony with Noah, a man who was far more likely to tempt me away from my goal. My heart still constricted every time I visualized his piercing blue eyes drawing me in from under his cowboy hat.

Ralph, who had stopped at the bar on our way in, walked up to the table juggling three beers. Setting them down in front of the women, he squeezed into a chair between Penny and me. Noticing he hadn't bought one for himself, I took it as a hint that I still hadn't cleared my debt with him for the motorhome's paint job. "What would you like?" I asked when he glanced over at me.

"How 'bout a pale ale." He draped his arm over the back of Penny's chair.

Wondering if and when my IOU to Ralph was going to expire, I took a seat at the end of the bar. As busy as the place was, it was going to take a few minutes to get the bartender's attention. There were two of them, actually. One was a forty-something blonde woman who had waited on me before. She had a command of her territory that indicated she'd been at the libations business for a long time.

The other bartender was a brawny middle-aged man with a full crop of salt and pepper hair. He didn't move as quickly, mostly because he served up drinks with a healthy dose of chatter. From the laughter surrounding him, the patrons preferred it that way. Listening to his Irish accent as his words rolled like silk from pour to pour, I gathered he was as much of an attraction as the Guinness.

"What are ya havin', darlin'?" he asked as he walked over and cleared an empty glass from the counter next to me.

"Two pale ales, please."

"Not from around here?" Moving to the set of taps just down from me, he pulled glasses from under the counter and began to pour my order.

"No, Southern California. But, you either." I smiled.

"You'd be right on that. Although, I expect you'll find far more folks around here from my lovely little island than from your homeland."

Thinking about the number of Irish accents I had heard over the past few weeks, I nodded in agreement.

"When I first set eyes on ya, I had ya for a Dublin girl." He set the beers in front of me.

"And why is that?" I handed him my credit card.

"All that red hair; reminds me of my own dear mamo."

Naturally. "Your mother?" I tried not to be too bothered by the comment.

"Grandmother."

"Your grandmother has hair this red?"

"She did, almost until the day she went to heaven, God bless her."

"I'm sorry."

"Don't be, darlin'. What a life she had, an angel with just enough of the divil in her to keep life craic."

"What?" Did he say crack?

"Fun." He smiled. "She never was one to settle for things as they was. She had a fine way of coloring them up. I'll bet you've a wee bit of the divil in ya too." He winked and walked away with my credit card.

I didn't know about that. Any devil in me was a wimp compared to the guilt-inflicting angel riding on my shoulder. That angel had confined me to a safe life for so long, I thought

I'd never find the audacity to get out. Maybe it was the devil rearing his head that prompted the move to New York. If so, I say, *Go Devil*. I needed him to keep me from running back to the familiar–or Noah.

"Will ya be with us long, Sydney?" The bartender read my name off the card as he handed it to me with the receipt.

"I've moved here."

"Well, isn't that fine news." He held out his hand for me to shake. "Carrick Hogan."

"Not Bridie O'Brien?" I asked, my hand lost in his thick fingers and strong grip.

"Ah, no." His eyes smiled as they met mine. "I'm no Bridie. Too much stubble." He rubbed his jaw and laughed.

Confused at first, I finally understood. "Oh? So, Bridie's a girl's name."

"Indeed."

"She's the owner, then?"

"No. 'Tis me."

"So, Bridie?"

"Just a girl in me dreams."

"Well, she has a lovely name." I smiled.

"Thank you, love."

"Nice to meet you." I picked up the beers.

"The pleasure's all mine. What a delight it'll be to have that fine red hair and those brilliant green eyes of yours round here reminding me of me mamo."

"Your grandmother, huh? Thanks," I said flatly.

"Tis a fine compliment, I promise ya. And, I promise when the rest of the men round here get a good look at ya, *they* won't be tinking of their mamos." He winked and smiled, his own devil in that grin.

"You *are* a charmer, Carrick Hogan." I smiled back.

"Just me way, darlin'."

CHAPTER THREE

After spending the evening listening to Ralph and his friends talk nonstop about the Yankees and cars, and Penny and her friends go on and on about reality TV characters as if they were personal acquaintances, I had enough. I slid my chair back and began to say my good-byes. Penny would have none of it.

"You can't leave now!" She looked down at her cellphone to check the time. "Malachi is on in ten minutes."

Tilting her head from side to side, Leeza added in a singsong voice, "You won't be sorry."

"He's the most mackadocious babe in the borough!" Courtney stood up and flipped her chair around to face the stage, which was only an arm's length from her, and then wriggled her bottom back into it.

Looking over at the men, I wondered how they felt about her comment, but they hadn't heard a thing. They were still too busy planning for the next baseball season, when the World Series hadn't even finished up on this one. I guess if the Yankees weren't in it, the season was over for them.

Okay, so Penny and her friends were right. Malachi was stunning–a perfect balance of masculinity and sensitivity. He was tall, dark-haired, and dark-eyed, with a square jaw covered in enough stubble to suggest virility, but not shoddiness.

Penny and Leeza turned their chairs around and slid them next to Courtney's. The three of them spent Malachi's entire set trying to draw his attention with their heaving breasts, naked legs, and overly enthusiastic applause. It was embarrassing, at least for me, who had spent most of my life trying to draw the attention away from myself. I was just thankful I had remained pulled up to our table, away from the other women.

I thought I had caught Malachi looking at me during his performance, but I realized that was ridiculous. He couldn't possibly have seen much of anything past Penny and company, especially with a stage light shining on him.

When he finished his set, I stood up right away, not wanting to extend the evening any further. The women were occupied with fawning over Malachi–there was no missing Courtney's high nasally voice and giggles–so it was the perfect opportunity to disappear. I started to give Ralph a sign that I was leaving, when Penny called my name. Darn.

Sighing inside, I started over to the group.

"You weren't going, were you?" Penny met me part way, clapped her hand around my forearm, and reached her mouth up to my ear. "You need to meet Malachi. I think he's really into you."

"What?" I pulled back. "No."

"Didn't you see the way he was staring at you during the show?"

"No." I pretended I hadn't because there had to be nothing to it.

"Well, he was. He's interested. I could tell. Come, come."

When I hesitated, she added, "What else do you have goin' on, girl? You plan on spending the rest of your life locked away like a nun?"

"No." I frowned.

"Then, let's go. It's Malachi," she said, so reverentially you would have thought I had drawn the golden ticket for an audience with the Pope.

With her hand still gripping my arm, Penny practically pulled me over to the group. Squeezing between Leeza and Courtney, she cut into the conversation, "Sydney, this is Malachi."

Reaching around Penny, because I was still partially wedged behind her, I held out my hand. "Nice to meet you."

He grasped mine for a few seconds beyond the normal greeting, while smiling at me with his eyes. "A pleasure."

"Syd-a-ney is from California," Courtney spoke up, looking over her shoulder at me, but not giving an inch of ground to allow me to move fully into the circle. Just as well. I wasn't staying. He was all hers.

"Really now, not originally from Ireland?" He studied my face. At least he had the courtesy to leave my hair out of the discussion.

"See, I told you he'd think you're Irish." Penny nudged me with her shoulder.

Uncomfortable that Malachi now knew he had been the subject of a previous conversation, I hoped the lighting was dark enough to hide any pink in my cheeks. "No. I've never been to Ireland, but Carrick thought the same thing."

"You've been talking to Carrick, have you? Well, you do give us a mind of the girls from home. Is your family from Ireland?"

"No. My ancestors on my grandmother's side were from Wales."

"Well, I suppose, we can find it in our hearts to forgive you for that."

"That's decent of you."

Anxious for the conversation to turn back to her, Courtney tossed her hair like she was making a shampoo ad and asked, "Are you going to be hanging here for a while?"

He set a twinkling eye on me for a split second before he turned to her. "That depends on Syd-a-ney."

I pretended to be interested in something behind me in order to hide my grin.

"What?" Courtney drew her eyebrows together.

"I'm wanting to hear more about these Welsh ancestors of hers, what do you say Syd-a-ney. Will you be havin' a pint with me?"

Shifting my face back to neutral, I glanced over at Courtney, who was looking none too happy with the turn of events.

"Oh, there's Gary and Evan waving to us," Penny said, running interference. "They told me they want to get together at the shore on Columbus Day weekend." She put her hand through the crook of Courtney's arm and herded her toward Leeza. "Let's go see what they're planning and decide if we want to commit."

As they walked away, Courtney pointed her nose to the ceiling and added some extra sway to her hips. Penny glanced over her shoulder and winked.

Great. I looked over at Malachi, hoping he hadn't noticed. He had. "Pushy."

"She has your best interest at heart, you can be sure."

"Right." I felt like I had lost control of the evening–because I had. In seeking a change in my life, I was determined to be the mistress of my own destiny, and yet every breeze that blew my way was still buffeting me.

"Take a seat here." Malachi pulled out a chair at a small table near us. "I'll fetch the pints."

Malachi returned shortly, set the beers down, and took the chair opposite mine, facing the bar. With the noise volume of the room still on high, it would have been easier to talk if he had scooted his chair closer. Leaving that wide a chasm of personal space between us indicated he wasn't as "into me" as Penny thought.

"What brings you to New York, Syd-a-ney?" Malachi adjusted his chair so he could stretch his legs to the side of the table.

"You need to stop with the Syd-a-ney, or it might stick." I smiled. "It's Sydney."

"What you be doin' here, Sydney?" He smiled back.

"I decided it'd be a good place to look for work as an editor, because there are a lot of big publishing houses based in Manhattan. Ralph's my cousin." I turned my head in the direction of the table where he and the rest had moved. "He offered to let me stay in his basement apartment." Not at all sure about Malachi or his intentions, I thought it best to stick with the short version of the story. The long version wasn't really all that interesting anyway. "How about yourself? How did you end up here?" I ran my finger down the condensation on my glass.

"Work too. It seemed more promising this side of the pond," he answered but with his attention focused behind me rather than on me.

"So, you're a full time musician?" With his eyes still drawn to something over my shoulder, he didn't respond. I asked again, this time a little louder. "Are you a full time musician?"

He finally looked back at me. "No, it wouldn't pay the rent."

"What's your day job, then?"

There went his eyes again, back over my shoulder. Jeez. What was with the guy? "Beg pardon?" he said when it dawned on him I had asked another question.

"Your day job. What's your day job?"

"A bit of this and that." He pulled his glass toward him, but didn't take a drink. In fact, he had hardly touched his beer.

Could he have been more vague? With his lack of attentiveness, I was quickly running out of curiosity about the man. I should have left him to Courtney. Looking down at my glass, I wondered how much of it I would have to drink before I could politely bug out of there. Mr. Bumbles and Alice were waiting at home, and they were a whole lot better company.

"Have you been to Wales, then?" he asked after moving his eyes beyond the bar area and scanning the entire room, and after enough time had passed that it finally dawned on him I was still sitting there.

"No."

"Not much of a traveler?"

"I just drove a motorhome all the way across the country to get here."

"Really? Why?" He straightened up, pulling his legs back under him, for the first time showing a glimmer of attention to our conversation.

"The RV was an inheritance from our uncle. Ralph wanted it, so I traded it to him for a few months' rent."

"Hmm." There went his eyes wandering off again. Not an exciting enough story, I guess.

Okay. I'd had enough. "Well, this has been great." I took a sip of my beer and set the glass down. "But, my dog hasn't been out in several hours. I need to get home." Reliable old Mr. B. He was always there when I needed him, even if just for an excuse.

Not seeming heartbroken at all, Malachi put up an obligatory protest, "Ya have to leave so soon?"

"Yeah, I really do need to go." I slid my chair back and stood.

"Let me walk you out." Malachi stood up also.

"That's not necessary."

"No trouble." He stepped around the table, put his hand on the small of my back, and started guiding me toward the door.

Okay, so what's this about? I pulled my purse higher up on my shoulder. Now, he suddenly becomes considerate? Weird.

As we passed by the table where Penny had moved, she looked over at me and smiled, clearly excited at the prospect of my leaving with Malachi. Pursing my lips, I gave my head a slight shake, hoping she would get the message that there was absolutely nothing going on. Courtney looked over also, and with forced indifference she turned back to the man sitting next to her and giggled loudly.

Stepping into night air that held a hint of winter, I folded my arms, pulling them to my chest. "Brr. It's going to take me awhile to get used to this weather. At home October can be one of our hottest months. Lots of fires too."

"Home?"

"Yeah, home. Los Angeles." I watched two young women get out of a car that had pulled over to the curb.

"But, isn't this your home now?"

"Well, um." I looked back over at him confused by the question, or at least in my own hesitancy to respond. Was this my home?

"It's been a delight, Sydney." Malachi reached for my hand and covered it in both of his, his brown eyes dancing as if he had just told an inside joke. "Goodnight."

"Goodnight." I turned toward the street, totally confused. Who was this guy? After checking for traffic, I glanced over my shoulder thinking Malachi would already be back in the pub. I was wrong. He was just disappearing around the corner of the building and down the alleyway that ran next to it. Who was this guy, indeed?

CHAPTER FOUR

After I put my purse down and grabbed a warmer sweater, I leashed up Mr. Bumbles to take him on a quick stroll around the block. As a Basset Hound, he wasn't exactly what you'd call an active dog, but he was always excited at the prospect of getting out. You could tell by his smile and the quantity of drool rolling off his tongue.

It was slow going, since Mr. B liked to evenly distribute the pee he saved up. As we finally turned the corner, I noticed two people in conversation on the next corner up from us. Although it was dark, there was enough light from the streetlamps I was pretty sure that one of them was Cork Feet. I couldn't see the shoes, but his posture and baseball cap were familiar.

Pretending to be absorbed in walking Mr. B from bush to bush, I moved closer, but stayed far enough away that I wouldn't draw attention to myself. I couldn't say for certain it was Cork Feet, but their movements looked a whole lot like that of the exchange I had witnessed outside Ralph's house. When it was over, Cork Feet hurried off down the street that paralleled Ralph's. The other guy walked diagonally across the intersection and faded into the darkness.

Tugging Mr. B away from his current sniffing target, I picked up our speed. If the twerp turned out to be a drug dealer, I thought it would be helpful for the authorities to know his comings and goings. The way I ended up appointing myself the Neighborhood Watch Committee of One spoke to the lack of effort I had made to broaden my horizons since moving to New York. And, the pub didn't count, especially after tonight. Sad.

When I reached the corner, through the darkness I could just make out Cork Feet walking up the steps of a house in the middle of the block. Slowing to Bumbles pace to remain inconspicuous, I made my way toward it. In front of the house next door was a large tree where Mr. Bumbles and I stopped so he could sniff and I could spy. Not that unlike Ralph's, Cork Feet's house was a brick two-story with white trim and a basement apartment. If my calculations were correct, it probably backed up to Ralph's, or at least it had to be close.

Thinking that it was late and I had done enough snooping for the day, I started to continue my loop around the block, when a van pulled to a stop in front of Cork Feet's house. Tightening Mr. B's leash, I moved back to the cover of the tree and watched as a half dozen people alighted from the van, speaking quietly to each other in what I thought was Spanish. Instead of walking up the steps to the front door, they walked single file around my side of the house and into the backyard. Before the last person from the van disappeared, she looked over at us, her attention drawn by the jingling of Mr. B's leash when he started scratching behind his ear. She stood frozen for a few seconds, then hurried after her companions.

Now, what was that about? The activity around Cork Feet was getting odder by the minute. Between Malachi's behavior at the pub and this latest sighting of Cork Feet, it had been one strange night. It was so disorienting that my homesickness knot had a tighter grip on my stomach than ever. When I found myself longing for the familiar faces of Harmony I knew that things had taken a decidedly perplexing turn.

On Saturday morning, after scrounging through my sorry little kitchen cupboards, I realized there was more food for my pets than for myself. Not really in the mood to go through the hassle of arranging for a taxi to take me on a major shopping outing, I decided to try the small market I had passed several times on my walks to the park.

As I approached the store, I took in the barred windows and peeling gray paint of the façade, thinking it wasn't the most inviting place I had ever shopped. I ventured in anyway. As my eyes adjusted to the dim lighting, I realized there was not another person in there, including the clerk.

I grabbed a basket from the stack next to the door, figuring someone would eventually show up. Perusing the aisles, I was careful to check the date stamps on the items, because some of the stuff looked like the expiration dates had long passed. I managed to come up with enough of my staples–Fritos, yogurt, cereal, almond butter, and bread–to last me until I was motivated enough to get to a supermarket.

As I approached the checkout stand, I heard the creaking of stairs. I looked over my shoulder to see an eighty-something man, with nothing covering his chest but a lot of gray hair, walking toward me carrying a shotgun. Holy cripes!

I quickly calculated the distance to the door, in case I needed to drop everything and run.

"Lo." He casually stepped behind the counter and bent down to place the gun on a shelf.

"Hello." I gripped tight to the basket handles.

"You want to purchase those things, young lady?" He nodded at my hand.

"Oh." I set the basket on the counter. "Sure."

As he started pulling them out, my curiosity got the best of me. "Aren't you worried that with leaving the store unguarded someone might come in and steal something?" I wanted to add, and where are the rest of your clothes, for goodness sake? He needed to keep his man boobs to himself, honestly.

"Nah." He pressed on the keys of his ancient cash register. "Cameras."

"Cameras?"

"Yah. They're all over the place. Could see every move you made."

Okay. That was just creepy.

"There's the gun too." He patted the counter. "I've been here a long time. People know not to test me."

"Is there much crime in this neighborhood?" I asked, thinking that as the local vigilante he may know something about Cork Feet.

"No more 'en the usual." He started putting my things into a paper sack. "That'll be $19.60."

When I held out my credit card, he shook his head. "Nah. Cash only."

"Oh, okay." I set my purse on the counter and opened my wallet. I'd have to keep that in mind for the future. Although,

I doubted I'd be much of a regular customer. I directed my eyes away from his chest.

After he handed my change to me, he turned toward a hat rack behind him. He pulled a plaid shirt from it, put his arms into the shirt and started buttoning it up. Thank God.

Now that he was clothed I thought I might be able to stomach continuing my probe into the neighborhood's illegal activities. "What kind of usual crime?"

"A bit of burglary, some drugs." He tucked his shirttails into his pants.

"You ever notice a young man around fifteen or sixteen years old, with a blue baseball cap and shoes that look like they're made out of cork, who appears to be dealing drugs?"

"That'd be Brandon Moran that's got those shoes."

"So, you know him?"

"Seen him around. Know his dad, Martin. Comes in here every day to buy his beer. Why you interested? You a narc?" He held his faded brown eyes on me.

"No. I've just noticed Brandon with other people, looking like he's dealing drugs."

"You sure?"

"No. I'm not sure. That's why I was asking *you* about it." Jeez, what was with this old guy, acting suspicious of *me*?

"Well. I wouldn't know. Never caused me no harm."

"But, he may if his drug dealing escalates into bigger crimes." Now he was making me mad.

"You just said you weren't sure if he *was* dealing. You new around here?" He pulled out a toothpick from the register and started sliding it through his bottom teeth. Yuk. Time to go.

"Yes. And, I'd like to think I moved into a safe neighborhood." I picked up my sack.

"It's up to you to protect yourself, young lady. No one else in this country's going to do it for you."

Wasn't that what I was just trying to do? Looking at him with that toothpick stuck between his teeth, I realized talking to him was an exercise in futility. I pulled my purse up on my shoulder. "Well, bye."

"Yah." He turned back to his register, pulled a key from his front pocket, and locked it.

After putting my groceries away and taking Mr. B on a quick walk, I decided to talk to Ralph about Brandon Moran. I saw Ralph's car out front, so I knew he was home.

He answered the door with a beer in his hand and led me back to his den. The TV blared with talking heads from ESPN, analyzing the latest sports news to death.

"Ya want one?" Ralph held his bottle out to me.

"No thanks." I was pretty sure it wasn't even noon yet. But, it *was* Saturday.

"How's it goin'?" He gestured for me to take a seat on the opposite end of the couch.

"Pretty well. No problem keeping up with my work without a lot of other things on my plate right now."

"Looks good with the boss, right?"

"I suppose. How about your work?" I had never asked him about life in the auto supply business. "You happy doing what you're doing?"

"Oh sure. There're a few headaches, but I've been there so long now I pretty much can call my own shots–which means weekends off to kick back." He tilted his bottle up and drank down the last of his beer.

"Great." I imagined that kicking back was Ralph's number one priority. I pulled my legs up under me and brought the conversation around to the real reason for my visit. "I've been seeing some strange activity around the neighborhood."

"Oh, yeah?"

"Yeah. There's a teenage boy I think is dealing drugs. I saw an exchange in front of the house here, one in the park, then one again around the corner last night. You ever notice anything like that?"

Pressing his lips together, he thought for a few seconds. "No. I don't think so."

"The boy wears cork shoes and a blue baseball cap. You've never seen him?"

"No. This is a pretty quiet place. If we were in the projects, now there, I'd believe it."

"So, you told me."

"I think he lives right behind you here." I stood up and walked over to the window that faced his rear yard.

"Oh, yeah?" Ralph didn't bother to follow me over.

"You ever notice people walking behind your house?" Looking out the window I tried to figure out if the house behind Ralph's was the same as the one I was in front of the night before. It was tough because most of the homes on both Ralph's block and the one behind his were made of brick with the same white trim.

"No," Ralph answered now focused on the television.

I walked back over to him. "The old guy in the market a couple streets up says the kid's name is Brendan Moran and his dad's name is Martin."

"Doesn't sound familiar." He dragged his eyes away from the TV.

"How long have you lived here?"

"Ten years or so. Yeah, I think ten years is about right."

"Do you know the old man who owns that market?" I sat back down on the edge of the couch.

"Chester Higgins?"

"I guess. He's about eighty, carries a shotgun, and doesn't wear a shirt."

That one got Ralph's attention. "Ha!" He laughed. "You definitely met Chester. He's the neighborhood libertarian."

"I gathered that."

"He's harmless."

"I don't know about that. The gun looked pretty real."

"I wouldn't worry about him."

"I won't. I don't think I'll be seeing much of him. I won't be shopping there."

"Good prices on beer, so long as you've got cash." He stood up and headed for the refrigerator, the word *beer* having triggered a Pavlovian response.

I took my leave, realizing that any conversation with Ralph about Brandon was not going any further than it had with gun-toting Chester.

When I opened my email that afternoon, there was one from Dori Hunt, a determined young woman I had met in Harmony. She had since moved to Los Angeles to start a new life away from a past that included a childhood reared in polygamy. She spent the years since she escaped that life helping other women escape from it also, but had her fill of Southern Utah and decided to move on.

I was happy to hear she had enrolled her brother Luke in a great school, with a program to assist him with social skills and sensory issues. He was a bright sixteen-year-old with special needs, but a lot of potential. Dori had to put off her own schooling until the following semester. She was working at a restaurant owned by a friend of Harry's, my ex, and also volunteering at a shelter for abused women.

With that homesickness ache still lodged in my gut, I decided that rather than send a return email I would call. Fortunately she wasn't working the lunch shift, so she picked up. After I caught her up on what I'd been doing, which took all of two minutes, I decided to give her a quick synopsis of the Brandon Cork Feet goings-on and see what she thought.

"First of all," she dove right into it, "those *were* drug deals. What else would they be? It wasn't like they were trading baseball cards or phone numbers."

I smiled. There was no uncertainty with Dori. Her life up until very recently had restricted her to Harmony, but so far as I could tell, her mind had never been confined. She sought knowledge on any number of topics and dispensed what she learned with gusto.

"And if that Chester guy specifically mentioned that Brandon's dad buys beer *every day*, I guarantee you he's not paying a whole lot of attention to his son. Do you know if there's a mom?"

"No. I didn't ask."

"I doubt it, or if there is one, she's working too long hours to be watching her kid, or is drinking along with her husband."

"What's your take on those people I told you I saw going into Brandon's backyard last night?" I moved over to the couch, sat down and put my feet up on the coffee table. Alice immediately sat up from her prone position on the chair across from me. She licked her belly twice, jumped down, then up on my lap, stretching out the full length of my thighs. Well, excuse me, Alice. Glad I can be of service. I scratched her behind her ears.

"Were they speaking a foreign language?"

"Yeah, Spanish, I think. But, they were whispering."

"If they were renters, wouldn't you think they'd be using the front door?"

"I suppose."

"And, why so many of them? Did they look like college students?"

"No. I don't think so. They would have been a lot louder."

"So, here's the thing ... hang on, wait a second." I could hear her muffled voice talking to Luke.

"Had to make sure he set the timer before starting on his video game or he'd never stop. Anyway, if Brandon is dealing drugs, he, or more likely his dad, could also be dealing in trafficking. They go hand in hand."

"You mean like sex trafficking?" I plied Alice from my lap, set her on the ground and sat straight up. Whoa! I wasn't expecting that.

"Were they all women?"

"No. It was a mix."

"Could be labor trafficking. Either way it sounds suspicious enough that you should keep an eye out."

"Labor trafficking?"

"Yeah, forced labor. There's a ton of it in this country, and especially in places like L.A. and New York. You might want to check with one of the groups in your area that deals with it."

"Okay, any suggestions on where to begin?"

"The Internet, and I'll ask a woman I know at the shelter who also works with victims of trafficking. Maybe she knows someone in New York you can talk to about it."

"Okay. Good. I think." I hesitated.

"You'll be fine. Just don't do anything stupid like approaching Cork Feet on your own. They can get very violent protecting their goods."

"Drugs?"

"Slaves."

"Wow!"

"Yeah, wow! I'll email you with that info when I get back from the shelter tomorrow afternoon."

Oh boy. I set the phone down. Well, I was looking for something to fill my time other than editing and walking a dog.

CHAPTER FIVE

Walking between the other copy editors' workstations on my way to the one I was assigned, I noticed my boss Collette Simmons blocking the entrance to the cubicle opposite mine. She was a petite woman in her early forties, with pumps to match every one of her formfitting suits. As I slid into my desk, I couldn't help but overhear the reaming she was giving that copy editor, whose name I had forgotten two seconds after she told it to me.

I have a terrible habit of not listening when introduced to someone. And, I consider myself a people person, too. I tell myself to use memory devices to help with retention, then I forget them. It's embarrassing.

On Mondays when we were both in the office I kept thinking I would hear someone else say her name. With the aid of Collette's not-so-petite voice, that Monday I did. Holly, that was it. Holly, Holly, Holly. Just think of her all wrapped up in Christmas garland. Maybe that will help.

From Collette's chastising, it appeared that Holly was up against a deadline she had little hope of meeting, a hocus pocus no-no in the editing biz. After a few more lashes,

Collette turned on her high heels and poked her head into my cubicle. "Meet me in my office in ten minutes."

"Sure." I opened my computer and focused my attention on it, so as not to appear as if I had overheard the exchange. Hearing sniffling, I wondered whether to continue pretending to be absorbed in my work to save Holly's dignity, or to acknowledge her misery. With minding my own business a trait I had never perfected, I chose the latter.

"You okay?" I scooted my desk chair across the aisle and leaned into her cubicle.

"No," she answered into a tissue she held to her face.

"Fell behind, huh?" I walked my chair closer to hers. Her lapse was already out there, so I thought we might as well acknowledge the problem.

She nodded, and blew into the tissue.

"Any chance of catching up?"

"I don't know." She took a shaky breath. "Mama's been sick. I've been up with her the last few nights. It's all I can think about."

"I'm so sorry." Poor thing. She was a mousy young woman, with limp brown hair, and a plump soft body, who had probably never lived apart from her parents.

"I can't lose this job. I need the money to support my family." She wiped the tears from her eyes.

Assessing her personality, I wondered why she ever became a copy editor in the first place, with the constant pressure from deadlines. Studying her bent head, I said, "I need to get to my meeting, but afterward how about I take you to lunch? I'll help you strategize how to finish your assignment on time."

"Oh, gosh." She looked at me quizzically, as if an offer to help didn't come her way very often. "Okay, yeah, that would be great."

"What's your drop dead date?"

"Wednesday."

"Wednesday?" Oh boy. That may be a little problematic.

Going into my meeting I was expecting nothing but a positive assessment of my work. I had submitted it before the deadline, and I was very good at my job. I should have been. I had been at it for enough years. So, when Collette sat behind her large glass-topped desk, challenging several of my judgment calls regarding the writer's grammatical style, I wondered what was up.

"For the most part, you've done a fairly good job with this." She looked down on me. I wondered how that was physically possible when she was barely five feet tall. Then I realized that my chair was shorter than hers–a common ploy among those addicted to power and control. "It won't take much for me to fix the errors," she continued condescendingly. "You've only been here a few weeks. I'm sure it won't take you much longer to catch on to the exacting requirements of this publishing house."

Hmm. I watched her as she turned her computer screen away to signal the end of the meeting. She hadn't called me in on the first two assignments I had completed. What was up?

"I'll send the file for your next job out this afternoon." She picked up her phone, and checked her messages.

"Fine." I stood up from my chair and leaned slightly over her desk so that she could feel the full extent of my height. Two could play at that game. "Bye-bye."

"Bye." She looked up at me, and pulled back a tick before she stopped herself. Looking quickly down, she resumed scanning her phone.

On the way to lunch, Holly asked if we could make a quick stop at her apartment to check on her mama. When we finally reached the door to her place, I was breathing hard. It was a fourth-floor walk-up in a dingy brick building at the fringes of Midtown. As she unlocked the door, I wondered why she wasn't in better shape. A few times a day scaling those stairs was the only workout you'd need.

Opening the door a crack, she stuck her foot in first then slid through the opening. I slid in behind her. When three cats trotted up and started rubbing their bodies against her legs I understood. I wouldn't have wanted to chase them down the stairs either.

"Oh!" I flinched when a tabby joined them and started working on my legs.

"That's Buster. And this is Billy, Bernice, and Betty."

Holly was a *cat person*, partial to the letter B. Who would have guessed?

"Mama's probably in the kitchen." She walked down the short entry hall.

Following her, I discovered she was oh so much more than a cat person. She was a cat cuckoo. The hallway opened into a living room filled with cats. Were there even that many names that started with the letter B? Didn't New York have a law restricting the number of pets you could keep in a small apartment?

And the smell... There were litter boxes everywhere.

"There's my mama." Holly walked into the kitchen adjacent to the living room.

Huh? Looking past her, I saw no sign of her mother.

Squatting down in front of a pile of blankets stacked on the floor next to the refrigerator, she said, "How you doing today, Mama Kitty?"

Oh. Not mama, *Mama Kitty*. Moving over for a better view, I caught sight of the ugliest cat I had ever seen. Seriously. It was missing most of its fur, with only an occasional tuft of gray here and there. Its skin was covered in growths. Its eyes sightless. Its mouth toothless. "This is Mama?"

"Yes, my Mama Kitty. She's been with me since I was ten."

"I can tell. And all the other cats? Have you had them long also?"

"My family?" She looked over her shoulder beaming like a proud parent. "I've been taking them in for almost seven years now."

"Nice." I tugged on my bottom lip, pondering the madness that my helpfulness gene had landed me in this time. "So, this is the family you were saying you need to support?"

"Oh, yes. Without me, I don't know what would become of them. There are too many cats in the shelters to house them, and there are just not enough rescue centers."

"And, you're one of them?" I wondered why the city would allow a cat rescue operation to set up shop in a residential building.

"No. It's just me."

"People call you when they find strays, then?"

"No. I find them myself. I specialize in cats that have been abused."

"Commendable."

"Let me give Mama her meds, and then we can get going to lunch." Holly stood up and moved over to the kitchen counter, which was completely covered in stacks of cat food cans.

Oh my God, how am I going to get out of this one? I watched Holly administer to her sick cat. The poor thing would probably prefer to be purring away in Mama Kitty heaven, which sounded a whole lot less abusive to me than dragging out its suffering.

"I don't normally invite guests over," Holly said as we squeezed back through her front door, "but I could tell that you're a cat lover."

"You could, huh?"

"You have one, right?"

"Yes. Alice."

"I knew it!" Holly led us down the stairs, convinced she had found a kindred spirit.

I am a cat person. I trudged down after her, my shoulders slumped. A *cat person*. Unbelievable.

Lunch didn't feel nearly as surreal as our trip to Holly's apartment, and I was able to offer her some tips on how she could work more efficiently to complete her assignment by Wednesday afternoon. I told her there was no way she'd make the deadline if she worked from home. She needed to stay at the office into the evening, and be right back there, first thing in the morning. Not only would it help her finish on time, but her dedication was likely to be noticed by Collette.

She was in agreement. I just hoped for her sake she could stay away from her cats long enough to save her job. My most convincing argument was she had the lives of her precious felines resting on her shoulders. She liked that idea. Holly–whatever her last name was–friend to all felines. Woo hoo.

Dori had emailed me the name of an anti-trafficking organization with offices in SoHo. I decided to check it out after saying good-bye to Holly and telling her I would see her in the office on Wednesday afternoon to congratulate her on the completion of her assignment. One of my reinvention intentions over the last few months was to become a glass-half-full person. The results had been spotty, but it was still too early to give up on my acquiring an optimistic attitude. And, there was the remote chance that Holly would come through.

While I stood in the entrance of the non-profit waiting to be noticed, I glanced through wire baskets containing information sheets on human trafficking and services for victims. Behind it were several desks, two of which were occupied by young women, deep into conversations on the phone.

A fortyish man, with bed hair and tortoiseshell glasses that gave him that tousled professorial look that coeds fall for was at another desk, also on the phone. When he finally looked in my direction, he held up a finger to indicate he would be with me soon.

"I have a volunteer application form right here." He set the phone down and shuffled through a pile of papers. "Here it is." He pulled it out, stood up, and walked over to me. "You'll need to complete both sides." He set the paper on the counter and tapped it. "Let's see, I think there were pens ..." He separated two of the baskets, searched through them, then looked at me when he came up empty. "Do you have one?"

"Um, I'm not here to volunteer. I just have some questions."

"You're not Kim?"

"No."

"Oh. She said she'd be here at two, and it's two." He checked his watch. His befuddled nature fit right in with his professorial looks.

"Nope. Not Kim. Sydney Roberts." I held out my hand.

"Vincent Bettancourt." He shook it.

"Would it be possible to talk with you for a few minutes?" I asked, thinking I was going to get a no, as preoccupied as he was.

"Hmm." He checked his watch again. It wasn't going to have changed much. "Sure, you'll just have to excuse me when Kim does arrive."

"That's fine."

"Have a seat." He nodded to a row of three chairs placed against the entryway wall.

"Thanks." I settled into one.

"What can I do for you?" he asked after he sat down.

"I was talking to a friend about some activity I witnessed that seemed suspicious, and she said it sounded like it could be labor trafficking. She volunteers at a center for victims of abuse in L.A. She found out about your organization from one of the people who works there and suggested I run my concerns by you."

"What did you see?"

"I don't know exactly. I noticed this teenage boy in our neighborhood dealing drugs, I think, and on Friday night when I was walking past his house, I saw six people file into his backyard."

"Was he with them?"

"No. He'd gone into the house a few minutes before that."

"Why did that seem suspicious to you?"

"It was just odd. They were very quiet, like they were deliberately keeping silent, and the last one to walk by seemed fearful when she saw me watching her."

"I might have been a little worried myself if I had seen someone staring at me." His dark eyes brightened behind his glasses.

"True, but I'm really not that scary looking, am I?"

Rubbing the stubble on his chin and scanning my face, he smiled. "No, I suppose not."

"And, I had my Basset Hound with me. There's nothing scary about a Basset Hound."

He smiled broader. "Basset Hounds are definitely more lovers than killers."

He knew the breed. Must be a good guy. "Anyway, it made no sense that that many people would be walking silently into a backyard late at night."

"Are you sure that his family doesn't rent rooms and have a back entrance to access them?"

"I'm not positive, but my instinct tells me something isn't right."

"Then you should keep an eye on the house and the boy you were talking about, see if there's something more concrete to go on."

"If it was labor trafficking, what would I be looking for?"

"There would be someone other than a teenage boy handling them, maybe a tough looking man around the house on occasion, although the handlers try to stay invisible. There's an information sheet up there listing the ways traffickers keep their victims under their control." He nodded at the counter. "What about the boy's parents?"

"I don't know. The dad may be an alcoholic. I'm not sure if the mother's even around."

"That's not much information to go on, but traffickers could easily be supplying the boy his drugs. Listen, if you do see something more concrete," he turned so he was facing me, "don't even think about doing something yourself. Trafficking is a highly lucrative business, and traffickers are deadly if you mess with them."

"Would I call you?"

"The police department has a task force. The info is on one of the handouts on the counter. We mostly deal with the victims."

"Are there a lot?"

"More by the week. We can't keep up, and there are several other non-profits in New York working with victims of trafficking as well."

"Wow, I had no idea."

Checking his watch, he looked toward the door.

"No Kim?" I asked.

"No Kim. You sure *you* don't want to fill out that application?"

"I don't know what I could offer, and I live clear up in the Bronx."

"What kind of work do you do?"

"I'm a copy editor for a publishing company right now."

"Writer too?" He combed his hair out of his eyes with his fingers.

"Yeah. How'd you know?"

"A lot of editors are frustrated writers."

"You sound like you have some experience with that."

"Yeah. I'm writing a novel in my spare time. I'm on page seven."

Catching the glint in his eyes, I smiled. "I can relate. Page twenty-three for me."

"If you're a writer, you definitely have a skill set we can use. We have a website and newsletter that need articles and editing."

Oh boy. Now, what do I say? "Let me think about it."

"So, that's a no." He stood up.

He caught me. I felt like such a do-nothing. Here Dori could find time to work at a non-profit, along with waitressing and the responsibility of her brother, while I automatically went into *No!* mode whenever I heard the word *volunteer*. So much for the glass-half-full goal. "Let me take a look at those information sheets, read up on the trafficking issues, and I'll get back to you." My guilt got the better of me. After pulling my purse off the back of my chair, I stood also.

"Guilt is a great persuader, isn't it?" His eyes twinkled as he echoed my thoughts.

"Psychic, huh?"

"We're not picky about the motivation. We just appreciate the help." He stuck out his hand. "Nice meeting you."

"You too." I grabbed it, impressed with his candor. The hair and glasses didn't hurt either.

CHAPTER SIX

Late that afternoon when I returned from Manhattan, I decided to walk around to Ralph's backyard to see if I could figure out which of the houses that backed up to his was Brandon's. I planned to return after dark to see if I could find better evidence of illegal activity. I also planned to follow Vincent's advice and spy from a long enough distance away that any bad guys wouldn't see me.

Scanning the houses and yards in both directions, it became obvious that manicured gardens were not a priority for the residents of the neighborhood. There was a preponderance of shaggy grass, overgrown trees and bushes, with the occasional spent flowerbed here and there. I couldn't get used to the *no fence* thing in the East, because every Southern Californian I knew subscribed to Robert Frost's "good fences make good neighbors" philosophy, but it did make my mission a lot easier.

Honing in on a house to the left of the one directly behind Ralph's, I walked over to where I could get a good look at it. Focusing on the far side, I noticed a dirt path between it and the house next to it. The tall tree cresting over the roofs of both houses had to be the one Mr. B and I used for cover. That made the path the one the people used the night before. And that made it Brandon's house. Now what?

Moving back toward Ralph's, I was searching for a good vantage point for my stakeout when I heard talking on the small deck above me. It was Ralph and Penny, and the better term would have been arguing, although it sounded mostly one-sided. Apparently, Ralph had forgotten some kind of anniversary or another. I personally didn't get the whole celebrating every *first* event thing–first meeting, first date, first night together–who can remember all that stuff? Penny, I guess, from the way she was chewing on Ralph. I imagined him with his hands in his pockets, doing a lot of nodding.

How I was going to make my way around to the front without being seen was the problem. I didn't feel right about continuing to listen in on what should have been for their ears only. I decided if I walked close to the house, then made a wide arc as if I was coming from the direction of the neighbor's place, they'd think I had just gotten there.

"Hey, cuz," I heard when I reached the far side of Ralph's house.

"Oh hi, Ralph." I did my best to sound surprised when I looked up and saw the two of them standing at the rail of the deck, Ralph with a beer in his hand. "Hi Penny." I raised my hand in greeting. She waved back, not appearing to be in too bad a mood or concerned I might have heard them.

"What you doin' back there?" Ralph asked, cocking his head like a puppy dog.

"I've never been in your yard. Just thought I'd check it out."

"Not much there."

"You know, houses in California all have fences around their yards. So, is the part in the middle there," I pointed between his house and the one that backed up to it, "is that common area? I mean, would it be all right to walk Mr. Bumbles through there?" I thought I was brilliant coming up with the idea of a scouting mission for Mr. B, plus I could find out if when I ventured into other yards on my stakeout I'd be trespassing.

"Nah. Every house has its own yard. The property lines are kinda blurred with the overgrown plants and all."

"Okay. Good to know."

"What happened with Malachi the other night?" Penny set her elbows on the rail and leaned on them.

Looking up at her through the fading light, I shrugged. "Short and dull."

"Malachi? Really? How could somebody that hot be dull?"

"I don't know. Maybe it was just me. Good news for Courtney, though. You can tell her nothing happened."

"She'll be doin' a happy dance on that one." Penny pulled her phone out of her back pocket and started scrolling through it.

Is she going to call her right now? That was fast.

"I had a cancellation for tomorrow." She continued scrolling. "I was thinking you might wanna come in for that cut and blowout."

"Oh." My hand automatically flew to my hair, and I pulled down on the strands that were curling too far down my back. "Um, okay. What time?"

"Ten." She looked down at me, drawing her long-nailed index finger across her brow to brush her bangs out of her eyes. "You know, it's psychic night tomorrow at Bridie's. You been yet?"

"No. I missed that one."

"She's fantastic. I'm telling you."

"Who is it?"

"Rosa Belli. She can see, oh my God, so much of your future. She talks to the dead. It's unbelievable."

I caught Ralph behind her rolling his eyes. Apparently, there was a difference of opinion regarding Rosa Belli's ability to see into the great beyond.

"With this whole starting over thing that you're doin' she could really help you. You have to come."

Disturbed by the thought that Penny could be accurate about my insecurity regarding the course I had set for myself, I said, "I'm not sure I believe in psychics."

"Oh, you will. Just wait. She starts doing readings at eight. But, you can't get there too late. She's very popular." Penny pulled away from the rail and looked down at her black sweater and pants. They were spotted with dirt. "Ralph!" She turned to face him. "Look at me!" She brushed at the spots. "I'm a mess. You need to get off your ass once in a while and clean this place, really!"

Not wanting to be a bystander to another argument, I held my hand up in a good-bye I'm sure neither one of them saw.

Later that night, a little before the time I had seen the people file into Brandon's backyard, I walked through Ralph's using the small LED light on my keychain to guide my way. Positioning myself behind a tree on the next-door neighbor's property, but well away from their house, I released the button on my light and leaned against the trunk to wait. It was late enough and dark enough that I was confident no one would be able to see me.

My plan was to stay put until I heard voices. Beyond that, I didn't know what the hell I was going to do. After about twenty minutes and with the October cold seeping through my cotton sweatshirt, I began to question my sanity. What difference did it make to me that some punk teenager was dealing drugs? But then, there was the whole labor trafficking thing. What if people were being held against their wills right there in the Bronx? I decided to stay a few more minutes.

Hearing footsteps on loose stones before I heard voices, I crouched down and moved around the tree. Unable to discern any more than mumblings, I duckwalked between two bushes. Still not close enough, and with my long legs burning from my squatting position, I stood up but remained bent at the waist while I took a few small steps closer to Brandon's house. By then, the people had made their way through the yard, and from the sound were ascending a set of outside stairs.

Spanish. They were definitely speaking Spanish. But, what did that prove? There are a whole lot of Spanish speakers in the U.S. Thinking I should try to get a look at them, and noticing a light from the second story, I took another step and glanced up at the stairway landing. A male figure stood silhouetted against the glow from the house. His whispers traveled over the night air as he greeted each person in Spanish when they passed by him and through a back door. He was wearing a hat, but it looked more cowboy than baseball, which had me confused. Caught up in trying to figure out if it was Brandon, I started to move closer, but as I set my foot down, I stepped on a twig that cracked loud enough to reverberate through the yards.

Shit! The voices on the stairs stopped, except for that of the man on the landing, whose whisperings became intense commands. Watching in horror as the last of the people scurried into the house and the man began to descend the stairs, I turned to flee. Conscious of not wanting to make any more noise, I focused my eyes downward through the dark and quickly picked my way through the bushes.

A cold chill crawled up my neck when I heard footsteps behind me. Noticing the vague form of Ralph's deck, I felt a flash of relief, thinking I might make it to safety without being seen. That relief turned to terror as I heard a second set of footsteps much closer. A moment later, a tall presence lunged up, bound me in his arms, clasped a hand over my mouth and pulled me along.

Hearing nothing but the loud pulsing of my own heartbeat in my ears, I didn't put up a fight. I couldn't. I was weak with fear, and the guy's grip was a vise of testosterone-forged muscle and determination. So much for all those self-defense classes.

When we reached the house next to Ralph's, my captor walked me through an open cellar door at the back and down a short set of cement steps. Pausing halfway, he pulled it shut without making a sound, with me still fast in his grasp.

That was it. The end. I was going to die right there in a cellar in the Bronx. But not before I was raped and tortured, by my best guess.

Guiding me to the back wall of the cellar, the man never loosened his grip on me. Quiet, except for the sound of our own breathing, we waited. It was apparent my captor was not going to initiate his macabre acts until the all clear bell went off in his head. It gave me time to think, and to plan my escape. Only there was no plan. The best I could come up with was to yell really loud and kick him hard in the nuts. I was as good as dead.

After a few minutes we heard the faint sound of footsteps pass by the cellar door, but they didn't stop. Thank goodness. Or not. A human trafficker or misogynistic murderer? In whose hands would I rather put my fate? Had I been able to pry myself free, I think I would have taken my chances with door number one–the trafficker. Or not.

Moot point, anyway. I wasn't going anywhere. And, of all things, I had to pee. Of course.

Enough time had passed that I questioned why we were still standing there. My racing heart, the smell of dank air, and the claustrophobic hold the man had on me made me light-headed. *Great.* How was I going to have a chance to defend myself if I fainted?

Maybe it was my trembling, but the man finally loosened his grip on me. "Keep quiet," he whispered into the back of my ear.

Right.

"Someone could still be outside."

I hope so.

"Okay, now. I mean it. Stay quiet." He whispered again and dropped his hand from my mouth.

My first reaction was, the hell with you, I'm screaming for help, but I didn't. I don't know why. It's what we learned in class. Scream and scream some more. Wow. To find out I would give up so easily, to find out I wasn't a fighter was likely my last self-recriminating thought ever.

I couldn't see my captor. I was too frightened to turn around and face him, and it was too dark. But I could smell him. And, it wasn't unpleasant, kind of like earthy shave cream–a scent I had smelled before. Where? And, why on God's earth was I thinking about shave cream when I was about to be drawn and quartered, or much worse? Is there such a thing?

"Don't move, Sydney, I'm going to check to see if it's clear," he whispered.

Right. Wait. What? He knew my name? Had he been stalking me? Even creepier. Who was he? I looked over my shoulder and stared hard through the blackness, but it was too dark to give me any clue.

"Wait here." He stepped away from me.

As he walked in the direction of the cellar door, I decided if I was going to have a chance to survive, I had to make my move then. Reaching into the pocket of my sweatshirt, I grabbed my keychain and found the button for the LED light. Once he opened the cellar door, my plan was to blind him by shining the light into his eyes, and then slip past him into the open.

Feeling my way across the room, careful not to stumble into anything, I knew I was close when I heard the soft sound of his movements. Focused on opening the cellar door, he hadn't heard me come up behind him. It was time.

Pressing the button, I lit up the stairway. Startled, he turned around, and I aimed a stream of light directly into his eyes. He drew the crook of one arm across his eyes to shield them and let go of the door.

Continuing to think of the light as my only protection, I kept it focused on him. I had precious seconds to get by him if

I was going to do it. Ready to shove, kick, and scream if he tried to stop me, I started up the steps.

He dropped his arm from his eyes and reached out to grab me as I passed him.

I opened my mouth to yell for help, but stopped, stunned in disbelief.

There standing before me was Malachi Keane, Irish singer–and serial killer? Huh? "Malachi?"

"Shush!" He reached out his hand to cover my mouth.

"No. You're not going to do this to me!" I slapped it away, thinking I sounded much braver than I felt.

"Shush!" He reached out again, this time with both hands.

Before he could trap me, I bent down, bit the back of his wrist, and started back up the steps with my hands up in preparation to throw the cellar door open.

In a flash, he had both arms around me, covered my mouth again, and dragged me down the steps.

My *mad* had finally kicked in. This time I didn't go quietly. Twisting from side to side, I tried to work myself out of his arms. No good. With my height I thought I had a chance, but he must have spent a lot of time at the gym when he wasn't singing and murdering people.

Finally wrestling me to a sitting position on the damp cellar floor, he pulled my arms behind me, and I felt the cold metal of handcuffs lock around my wrists. When he pried the keychain from my palm, the room went black again.

"What's the matter with you, you crazy woman?" He moved around in front of me and hissed through the dark, keeping one hand around my upper arm. "I'm here to help you."

"Sure, that's why I'm sitting here in handcuffs," I spat out. "And, what happened to your accent?" I would have known a whole lot sooner that it was Malachi if he had been speaking like he was fresh off the boat from Ireland. Not that it would've made him any less of a violent criminal, just one I knew liked to buy a beer for his victims before he plotted their demise.

"Would you just shut up, you eejit," he said in a loud whisper. "You may have destroyed seven months of work."

"You're calling me an idiot?"

"Just shush." He put two fingers to my mouth. "So we can get out of here."

"But ..."

"No." He squeezed my upper arm and moved back to the cellar door.

Seven months of work? What was going on? As my heartbeat started to slow and my flight or fight instincts gave way to my rational brain I considered the possibility that Malachi may not actually be a serial killer. But, *what* then?

"Okay," he said quietly as he returned and kneeled down at my back, "I don't think there's anyone out there. If there were, they would have been on us by now with all your shrieking."

"I wasn't shrieking." I felt his hands on my wrists.

"No. You were shrieking. And, you need to keep quiet." Removing the cuffs from my wrist, he put his hand under my elbow to help me to my feet. Thank God. The cold ground was making me stiff and had ramped up my need to pee.

Keeping his hand on my elbow, he led me up and out of the cellar, closing the door behind him. I decided to cooperate for the moment. I still wasn't sure if Malachi was friend or foe, but now that we were outside at least I had a better chance to escape if it turned out to be the latter.

When we finally reached the side of Ralph's house, he stopped, staying clear of the light from the streetlamps. "What were you doing back there?" he asked quietly, tugging on his belt to adjust it. It was the first time I noticed there was a holstered gun attached to it. Scary.

Pulling my eyes from the gun, my temper flared. "No!" I tried to keep my voice down, but it wasn't working very well. "You just attacked me, dragged me to a cellar, and handcuffed me. You don't get to ask any questions until I know what the hell is going on!"

He looked over my shoulder and then at me. "Okay, that's fair. But, I'm not at liberty to tell you much. I'm the lead investigator in a case involving criminal activity in the area."

"You work for the police?"

"Something like that."

"Not an Irish balladeer?"

"That too." He was only a silhouette, but I could hear the smile in his voice.

"You work undercover?"

"Yeah. And, I'd like to keep it that way. My turn now?"

"I guess."

"Why were you back there?"

I gave him a one-minute rundown on the drug exchanges I witnessed, and the activity I had seen around Brandon's house.

"You decided to take it upon yourself to go poking around where you knew there may be dangerous felons? You do know that had you been caught they would have gone very hard on you."

"And what you did to me doesn't count as hard?" I rubbed my wrists, feeling a bit defensive, when all I was trying to do was be a good citizen. Or, so I believed.

"You didn't give me any choice." I could just make out him moving his hand to his wrist. It was too dark to tell for sure, but I think there may have been teeth marks. "At least you would have given Cobo a good fight."

"Cobo?"

"The man who started after you. You would've lost, by the way. He's a nasty piece of work."

"Why don't you just arrest him, if you know what's going on?"

Uncrossing his arms, he locked his eyes on mine. "It's bigger than that, an ongoing investigation, and as such you need to stay out of it. I just hope you haven't jeopardized it already."

Feeling like I was being scolded, but still bristling enough from his treatment of me, I was able to ward off most of my usual absorption of guilt. "Do you think Cobo suspects someone was spying on him?" I looked over my shoulder at the yard.

"He might. At the very least, he's going to be extra cautious now."

"What if I see something?"

"As in, by chance, or as in continuing to place yourself in situations that can get you killed?"

"I'm not going to risk my life." I scowled at him, bothered that he thought I was that stupid. "But, I'm also not going to stay cloistered in the house. Mr. Bumbles would be one unhappy Basset Hound if he couldn't get out for his sniff and pee."

"Mr. Bumbles?" His crooked grin and smiling eyes reminded me of why Courtney was crazy for his attention. His was a classic strong-jawed face, with just enough of a cleft in his chin to raise the blood of any woman with a pulse.

"Yep. That's his name." I noted to myself that I indeed had a pulse, even though the guy had just given me the scare of my life. Forcing myself to turn my attention back to the bad guys, I repeated, "What do I do if I see something?"

"You can contact me through the number on this card." He reached into his pocket and handed it to me. "Just give your information to whoever answers the phone. It'll get to me."

"Fine." It was clear that at least as an investigator he planned to remain as far out of reach as possible. But as an Irish performer, I assumed he was going to keep his gig at Bridie's. Weird. "It's going to be strange running into you at the pub. It's kind of hard to think of you as a singer now."

"But, I am a singer, darlin', and so long as you don't bite me, it'll be grand." He reverted to his Irish accent.

"And, so long as you don't wrestle me to the ground." I frowned at him.

"Oh, I dunno about dat, love," he kept up the accent, "tis the most fun I've had on the job in a long while."

Uncomfortable at the comment, I was glad we were still in the shadows. Looking over Malachi's solid physique, much more evident than when he was holding his guitar, I felt relieved that the evening had ended in his company rather than that Cobo guy's. Taking a deep breath, I was suddenly very tired and well beyond my capacity to ward off a trip to the water closet. "I gotta go. Mr. Bumbles really *does* need to get out." Blame it on Mr. B. I started to move toward the front of the house.

"Wait just a minute." Back to his cop voice, he walked toward the street, but stayed close to the house, looking in both directions. When he returned, he said, "Okay, it's clear."

"Good. Thanks. It's been ..." I hesitated. What do you say about an event that was probably going to give me nightmares for years? "Memorable."

"Indeed."

"Bye." I raised a hand.

"Bye." He started toward the backyard. I guess his night wasn't over. Stopping, he looked back over his shoulder and said softly, "I'd like to meet that dog of yours sometime," and then disappeared into the dark.

CHAPTER SEVEN

Staring into the mirror, I was speechless.

Okay, I admit I liked the haircut and highlights. And, the blowout left my hair smooth and wavy–for now. However, it was hard to believe that tight spirals weren't going to break out all over my head any moment. Or, that it was safe to soak someone's hair in formaldehyde. That's right, *formaldehyde*, as in what they use to preserve dead bodies–something Penny casually mentioned *after* she applied it.

I also thought I might get used to the gold highlights. Penny promised they would enhance my natural cedar color. Maybe.

But, my face, what was I going to do about my face?

Penny thought I had missed the look of panic that crossed her own face when she unwrapped the cooling towels from mine. But, no way. I knew immediately something had gone very, very wrong with the *spa* facial she promised would, "OMG, change your life!"

Change my life, oh yeah. Because I was going to be spending the rest of it hiding in Ralph's basement with a bag over my head!

"It's totally going to calm down in a few hours," Penny was saying from behind my chair, her face a picture of composure above my own incredulous expression in the mirror.

Right. Turning my head from side to side, I looked for any spot that might have escaped the scalding from whatever *all natural* chemical she used. Not a one. She was thorough. I gave her that. The pink I had turned was ten times as intense as the color that generally accompanied the awkward moments of my life. And, there was absolutely no way it was going to "calm down" in a few hours.

"What am I going to do?" I asked far more evenly than I felt.

"Well, for now I'll apply some foundation," she said all perky-like. "It's one I sell to my older clients, a little thicker. And after a while you can go back to using your regular makeup."

Great! So, layered over my flamingo pink skin will be an inch-thick coating of heavy make up. Lovely.

"I'll do your eyes too," Penny offered. "You're going to look terrific, I'm telling you. Strangers will be complimenting your skin, I mean it."

"Fine." What else was I going to do?

After she finished using my face as a canvas for a makeover suited for a nineteenth century hooker, she patted my shoulders. "There now. Can't tell a thing. You look terrific. Ready for psychic night at the pub, girl?"

I'll fit right in–since I look like an otherworldly freak! "I'm not sure I'm going."

"But, you have to, Sydney," she whined my name. "I have like this sort of, you know, prickly feeling in the tips of my fingers." She held her hands out. "That you should go. When I get this, I'm always right. I'm a little psychic myself, you know."

A little *psycho*, maybe. Or, was I being my usual judgmental self, compiling a list of reasons *not* to like the New Yorkers I'd met, so if it didn't work out I would have concrete evidence to support my departure? Jeez. It had only been a few weeks, and I was already formulating an exit strategy. Not fair. I needed to give it more of a chance. New York was a huge change. I couldn't expect to feel at home yet. "Okay, can't ignore your Spidey sense." I gave in.

Drawing her thin arched eyebrows together, she looked confused.

"I'll go."

"Oh. Good." She combed her bangs across her eyes with her fingernails, looking genuinely relieved. She *was* a nice person. I just wish she had been better at her job.

Filled to the gullet with bodice-ripping rogues and bad grammar, I stood up from my computer and straightened my spine. I had been editing for hours, determined to meet the "exacting requirements" of the publishing house and deprive my boss Collette of the pleasure of staring down at me from her lofty desk chair.

Looking over at Mr. B, who was sprawled out on his side on the vinyl floor in the kitchenette, I contemplated disrupting his nap for a little exercise. As I turned back to close my laptop, I noticed Brandon's shoes through the transom window. What drew my attention as much as the return of

Cork Feet was he was toe to toe with black reptilian cowboy boots. It was an odd enough image that I decided to grab Mr. B and see what was going on.

Warning myself to keep totally engaged in Mr. B so as not to draw attention, I walked out my door and up the steps, pausing to pretend like I had to straighten the leash. Bending down, I slid my eyes up to where I could get a look at them. My heart quickened at the sight of the back of a cowboy-hatted head. *Noah!* No. My mind was playing tricks. Of course it wasn't Noah.

Oh, shoot, my heart clenched again, but this time in fear. It had to be the guy from the top of the stairs that Malachi had identified as Cobo. And, from his staccato movements and jabbing finger, he was none too happy with Brandon. The only thing I could make out of what was being said was something about *rock*. Slang for some drug? I didn't know.

Brandon kept trying to move back, but Cobo wouldn't let him out of his reach. It was the first time I had a chance to examine Brandon's face, and what I saw was a frightened boy, not a hardened drug dealer. He had gotten himself in deep, and he couldn't figure a way out. That's what I wanted to believe anyway.

Realizing how risky it was for me to be standing there, I took a moment to decide whether to sneak back into my apartment or to hurry off in the opposite direction before being seen.

It was one moment too long. Brandon pulled his eyes off Cobo long enough to notice me. Looking from me to Mr. Bumbles, his eyes widened.

Shit! Had the people from the other night described Mr. B and me to him, or had he just not seen a Bassett Hound before? He turned back to Cobo, and it wasn't two seconds before he snapped his head around to stare at me.

Double shit! The people had to have described us. What was I thinking bringing Mr. B? It wasn't like we blended in. And now they knew where I lived.

My only choice was to continue to act like I was just walking my dog and knew nothing. To validate that, I decided I would head in their direction rather than scurry off the other way. Trying to act as casual as possible–right!–and moving Mr. B over to the curb in conscientious dog walker fashion, I pushed my sunglasses up the bridge of my nose and focused on a white SUV that was passing by.

"Nice dog," Cobo said with a slight Latin accent, as I pulled even with them.

My God, my God, my God! I could have thrown up, but instead managed to say, "Thanks," not stopping, and avoiding all eye contact.

"You have a nice day, ma'am," Cobo said as I came even with him. Out of the corner of my eye I watched him nod his head like a polite cowboy. But, that man was no cowboy.

"Thanks." I pulled Mr. B along, for once wishing he were one of those hyper little dogs that drag their owners down the street.

"You're welcome," Cobo called after me, and then laughed. But, there was no humor in that voice. Just pure evil.

Fear crawled up my spine and settled at the base of my neck.

I hadn't been looking forward to psychic night at the pub, but now eight o'clock couldn't come fast enough. I was just praying for Malachi to be there. I wasn't going to trust this one to a phone call. I needed to see him. I needed help. I may not be psychic, but I knew Cobo wasn't about to leave me alone.

Psychic night was popular. The pub was packed. When I walked in I was expecting to see a stage set up with a microphone for Rosa Belli to use to do her readings, but there wasn't one. The patrons were gathered in garrulous groups around the bar and at tables, like any other night.

My experience with psychics was confined to reality TV, the kind you watch when you're home sick in bed with the flu. And, I didn't buy it. There was too much sleight of hand. The psychic would say, "I'm hearing from a spouse who recently passed on..." No kidding. How hard was that to guess, when the majority of the population is or was married? And I hated the way they played with people's emotions. The looks of vulnerability were hard to watch, especially when the psychic was wrong and covered for it by quickly moving on to another audience member.

"There you are." Penny squeezed her way past a group gathered by the door. "You look terrific." She twisted her head from side to side as she examined my face and hair.

I had to disagree. My face was so pancaked with makeup I could scratch my name in it. And my hair was rapidly furling from wavy to curly. I wished I had enough attitude to make dark sunglasses a permanent feature, but I couldn't pull it off. I, of course, told none of this to Penny. Wouldn't want to hurt her feelings. "Thanks."

"We're over there by the window." She looked over her shoulder.

"Where's the psychic show going to be?" I moved closer so she could hear me over the crowd noise.

"Oh, it's not like that, you know, not like those Vegas mediums." She stretched up so that her mouth would be closer to my ear. "It's better than that. She does *private readings*." She drew out the last two words for emphasis. I was supposed to be impressed.

"Here?" I wondered how Rosa Belli could tune into her dead people in that raucous place.

"Sure, she's in the back." She grabbed my hand. "We gotta get over there. The list is filling up."

"Oh, well, I…" I said to Penny's back, trying to let her know I really didn't need or want a private reading. She didn't hear me. She had me through the bar and on that list before I could get another word out.

I had the 10:45 slot. Goody, two and a half hours to chat it up with Ralph's merry little band. Okay, that was way too snarky. Wasn't I supposed to be giving New York more of a chance? And besides, I had to be there anyway to wait for Malachi to show up. That is, if he was going to.

After a few rounds of beers, I looked around the table at Ralph and his friends, admitting to myself that the evening had been kind of fun. They didn't run away in fright at my overly made-up face, or even seem to notice it. Maybe it was more the norm in the Bronx. I looked over at Leeza, wondering how many fake coal-black eyelashes she had glued over her own.

With no sign of Malachi I decided to ask the group if he would be performing, knowing full well it wasn't his usual night. Courtney perked right up on that, a look of suspicion moving across her eyes. I guess that Penny's report of my one very short drink with Malachi hadn't been enough to convince her I wasn't competition. With an attitude that implied she had exclusive knowledge of his every move, Courtney told me that on the nights he wasn't performing if he was going to stop in it was usually late.

And that's about all you know, girl. Flashes of the previous night and my encounter with Cobo still gripped me.

CHAPTER EIGHT

When it was time, I made my way to the back of the pub for my reading, keeping a lookout for Malachi. So far as I could tell, he wasn't there, but it was still a little early.

After waiting for a few minutes next to the panel screen that separated the psychic from the rest of the room, unsure of the procedure, a middle-aged woman in a New York Jets jersey came out. She told me it was my turn, and continued on to the bar.

I don't know exactly what I was expecting, a gypsy maybe, with a crystal ball, or a brassy broad with a thick New Jersey accent, but Rosa Belli was neither. She was thin and thirty-something, with brown hair and pale skin. Her ringless fingers were long and tapering, and they were the only part of her that was animated as she ran them over the wine-colored tablecloth in front of her.

Nodding to the chair across from her, she indicated I should sit down. After I was settled, she took a deep breath, closed her eyes for a few seconds, and continued to make circles with her fingers. When she opened them, she asked, "Why are you here?"

That was a good question, but answering that I was coerced didn't seem right. "My cousin's girlfriend told me about you. She thinks a lot of your abilities."

"No." She breathed deeply again. "Why are you here?"

Hmm. Okay? Was it a trick question? Existential? I asked for clarification, guessing she could tell I wasn't a local. "You mean, why am I here, as in New York?"

"Yes."

"I wanted a change."

"But, this isn't your place. You're not happy here."

How'd she come to that conclusion? Did I look unhappy? "It's only been a few weeks I don't know how I feel about New York yet. I can't say I dislike it."

"But, there's a place that gave you a sense of belonging."

"Los Angeles. Of course I felt like I belonged there. I lived there all my life. But, I grew discontented with it. I needed to discover what else was out there."

"No. It's not Los Angeles." She relaxed her face, focusing inward. "This is a dry place, with very little plant life. The people live simply. They're honest." She quieted her hands. "You connected with them."

If she was referring to dust-dry Harmony, it was definitely not all of them. But, how could she have known? "I *was* stuck in a town in the Utah desert on my way here, but only for a week. A week is not enough time to make meaningful connections." I was being a little dishonest as Noah's blue eyes sprang to mind.

"Time is not an element of the light that links souls," she said softly.

Okay? I needed a month on a mountaintop to contemplate that statement. "If I belonged there why did I feel like a fish out of water?"

"You weren't paying attention."

"But, there's nothing for me in Harmony. I can't work there."

"Then, you chose to close the door."

"On that place, yeah maybe, but not on *every* place. I plan to keep looking if New York doesn't work out."

She rested her eyes on mine. "What do you think you will find in this place?"

"I don't know, something to shut up the voice in my head that keeps telling me I should be doing more with my life, maybe." I was surprised to feel my jaw tighten and heartbeat speed up in anger. Where was that coming from?

"More what?" she said with the same soft patience she had maintained throughout our conversation.

"I guess I'll know when I find it." I shrugged my shoulders.

"Not if you close the door."

Unable to maintain eye contact with her, I looked at the lithograph of a tall ship on the wood-paneled wall behind her. Why was this conversation getting to me, and why did it feel more like I was talking to a shrink than a psychic? Time to end the session. I reached for my purse, which I had stashed under my chair. I hadn't asked how much the voodoo was going to cost. I hoped not a lot, because I sure didn't get my money's worth.

When I straightened back up, Rosa was making circles on the tablecloth with the fingers from both hands again, her eyes closed. When she opened them, they were smiling. "Your father said to tell you the shelves are stacked with every tool ever made and the air is filled with the scent of sawdust. Do you understand?"

I nodded, the hairs on my arms standing on end.

"And your mother says she wears a different pair of shoes every day. Do you understand?"

Shivering, I nodded again.

"They also want you to know they're sorry they left you so soon, but they're with you and have faith your path will be made clear. They said they're proud of how hard you've worked to make it on your own, but you need to lighten up a bit, to go easier on yourself."

Stunned, I held my breath, trying not to lose control of my emotions. The back of my throat stung, and I wasn't sure if I was going to get any words out without sobbing.

"Your parents understand you. Honor their memory by acknowledging they're still in your life, and by remembering their words."

"I will." Tears filled my eyes, blurring my vision of her.

I was so disoriented by the message from my parents that I wasn't sure what I paid her, or even if I managed to say good-bye. If she was a charlatan, she was a really good one. She could have found out from Penny that my parents had died, but the references to hardware stores and shoes? I don't know where that came from.

I was still trembling as I made my way past the bar. Looking across the room to see if Ralph and Penny were still there, I noticed Malachi at a table near ours. Courtney was sitting next to him, her chair turned toward his. She was leaning far into him, taking advantage of the chance to expose her considerable breasts. Great. It was going to be impossible to pry her away from him now that she had his attention.

Keeping Courtney's back to me, I walked toward their table. When Malachi finally noticed me, I nodded toward the door, hoping he would get the message that I needed to talk to him. When I saw him dip his chin in understanding, I turned toward our table and rejoined Ralph and his group, who were in weekend mode, even though it was only Tuesday.

After twenty minutes, I was thinking I would have to give up on talking to Malachi, which was not good news. I thought somebody should know that Cobo and Brandon had fingered me, in the event I ended up dead by morning.

Finally, both Courtney and Malachi walked over, Courtney with the attitude of someone who had scored a big one. So, when Malachi pulled away from her, she looked more like she had let the big one get away.

"Sydney said she'd help me edit the insert for my new CD," Malachi said to the table. "We won't be but a moment."

Scooting my chair back, I was careful to avoid eye contact with any of them. I had no poker face.

When we reached the office where Malachi kept his things, he turned on the lights and closed the door.

He started to speak, then stopped, staring hard at me with a quizzical look. Unlike those at my table, he had noticed my makeup.

"Penny's handiwork." I rolled my eyes, thinking that the only good thing about it was with foundation that thick he couldn't see the pink from the facial, or my embarrassment.

Cocking his head, he still looked confused.

"Penny, my cousin Ralph's girlfriend, is a hairdresser who insisted on giving me a facial today. Apparently, she missed that week in beauty college, because it didn't go so well."

"Right, then. What's up?" He immediately reverted to cop mode, satisfied with my reply, or more likely disinterested. I was okay with that. The last twenty-four hours had been absurd, and he was the only one who I could talk to about it. Not a bad thing. His aura of confidence was reassuring—and attractive.

"I'm afraid Cobo and Brandon may know I was the one outside their house."

"Why's that?"

I told him about my encounter with them that afternoon.

"It does sound like Cobo was taunting you, but that's his way."

"No. I know Brandon recognized me. I could tell. And, I have no doubt he told Cobo about me. What do you think I should do?"

He ran his fingers across the stubble under his lip. "At the very least they'll keep tabs on you to see if you're going to be a problem for them. So, you're going to have to keep far away from that bunch, right."

"But, what if they come after me?" I was unconvinced that staying away from them was all I needed to do.

"Your cousin lives above you?"

"Yeah."

"Put him on notice you're worried about a stalker or something like that, and that you'd like to be able to get a hold of him at the odd hour if necessary. Tell him you'd like him to keep an eye out for people who might be lurking about the house and the block. Ask him to check on you if he sees something that looks suspicious.

"But, he's not always home at night." I frowned, knowing he often spent the night at Penny's.

"Hmm." He looked down at his feet then back up at me. "I don't usually do this for people who have bitten me ..."

"What? You ..." I started to protest, then saw he was smiling. Nice to know he had a sense of humor. I smiled back, thinking that I *had* behaved like a mad woman the night before. But, he still wasn't off the hook.

"I'll give you my direct line in case you can't get a hold of Ralph, but emergencies only, right?" He reached into his pocket. "No calling anytime you feel like beating someone up."

"Agreed." I took the card. "Thank you."

"And really, girl, I mean it, leave the undercover stuff be. We've got it."

"Promise." I put his card in my purse.

Not wanting to walk home alone, I hung in there with Ralph and Penny to the bitter end. Malachi and Courtney had moved back to a table by themselves, a good thing, I guess, since it quashed the idea I was doing anything more for Malachi than helping him out with his CD.

Looking over at them when our group finally called it quits for the night, I wondered if he actually saw anything in her, or if it was just part of his cover. He didn't seem to object too much to her pawing. I watched Courtney rub his arm. What did I care? I knew what the guy did for a living, sort of, but that was about it.

Standing up and stepping back from the table, I bumped into Carrick, the pub owner. "Oh, sorry." I pulled my purse up on my shoulder.

"No worries, darlin'." He reached around me to pick up some glasses and set them on the tray he was carrying. "Did things not work out for you tonight?" He nodded his head toward Malachi.

He must have seen me staring at them–brother! "No, I uh, things are fine." I thought his comment was a little too personal, even for a philosophizing bartender with a sympathetic ear.

"It's just with you lookin' so fancy it's a wonder you don't have a man on your arm."

Oh no, he couldn't be serious. Calling the job that Penny did on my face fancy? Must be an Irish thing. How to answer that? "Your pub is quite a hub for the neighborhood." I decided it would be easiest to change the subject. "It's hard to make it in the restaurant business. You seem to have come up with a formula that works."

"I had a lot of experience before I opened this place. My father and grandfather before him owned the local in my village."

"Pub?"

"Aye."

"Well, you've done a great job." Wanting out of the discussion before he decided to bring up my love life again, I was relieved to see Penny and Ralph moving away from the table and heading for the door. "We'll be going now." I turned to follow them.

"Home to walk the dog, then?" Carrick asked.

I looked back at him, confused by his asking about Mr. B, when I was pretty sure that in our previous conversations I had never mentioned him. "How'd you know I have a dog?"

"Just a lucky guess." He winked.

"Okay." I pushed a chair aside to clear a path to follow Ralph and Penny. "Bye." I lifted the fingers of my right hand, a feeling of uneasiness dominating my frame of mind.

"I'll be watchin' for your return." He winked again.

Oh boy. I needed to get home to Alice and Mr. B. That was all too weird.

Standing outside of the pub, I waited for Ralph to say his good-byes to Penny. She had brought her car and was dropping Leeza off then going home, and Ralph would not be joining her. She had early clients, I heard her tell him, although early in New York, I was finding out, was relative. I was fascinated that many of the breakfast places in the city didn't open until nine on *weekdays*. In Los Angeles, by nine on weekdays most people would be cruising along at five miles an hour, worrying if they were going to be late for work or an audition.

As Penny and Leeza walked away, they were having a great time speculating about the details of Courtney's evening with Malachi and whether it would be an overnighter.

Ralph bumped his shoulder into mine, way too close for someone smelling that strongly of beer. "You know you coulda had him if you wanted."

"What?"

"Malachi. He liked you."

What was this, third grade? I put space between the two of us to avoid his lurching into me again. "No, Ralph."

"Sure. I saw the way he was lookin' at you."

"No. There's nothing there."

"There could be."

"No. There's nothing between us, and I wouldn't want there to be." This was definitely turning into a playground argument.

"But ..." He stepped in front of me and tapped his finger on my chest. "You don't need a worry. There's gonna be somebody come along for you real soon."

Jeez. I moved out of his reach. There went my opportunity to talk to him about being on the lookout for my "stalker." He was too damn drunk and too concerned about my love life.

We continued along in silence, thank goodness. Ralph had expended the last of his energy on the pep talk, and was slouching toward home, his hands in his pockets. A lot of good he was going to do me if I ran into Cobo and Brandon. I was better off on my own.

When we passed by the market owned by Chester Higgins, a middle-aged man with toothpick legs and arms and a belly he'd been growing for decades, walked out holding a large grocery sack. Chester, backlit by the fluorescent lights from the store, had been holding the door open for him. Mumbling, "Bye, Martin," he then nodded his head at us and let the door creak closed.

It must be Martin Moran, Brandon's father. Through the dim light of the streetlamps, I noticed his gait was about as steady as Ralph's. This was probably not his first resupply mission of the evening.

With him far into his bender, I thought I might be able to get something out of him without him remembering later. Stepping up my pace and leaving Ralph to linger along, I pulled even with Moran. "Evening," I said casually, as I pretended to be passing.

"Huh?" He shifted his parcel on his hip and looked over at me.

"Nice night."

"Hmph," he mumbled.

"I think you're my neighbor." I pretended like I had seen him before. "You have a son, right?"

"Yeah." He looked over at me again, his eyes unfocused.

"Brandon?"

"Uh, huh."

"Seems like an enterprising young man." I slowed to stay even with him, but far enough away that the darkness hid my features.

Coming almost to a spasmodic stop, he slurred, "He's a good son."

"How wonderful for you. Hey, I noticed you have renters, right? We were thinking of picking up some extra cash that way. How's that working out for you?"

"Hmph," he mumbled again, shaking his head like he thought it would help him make sense of what I was saying. "All right."

I had tested Moran enough. Drunk or not, I didn't want him to become suspicious. "Have a nice night." I bent down like I needed to tie my shoe–never mind that it didn't have any laces. I stayed that way while Moran continued down the street and Ralph caught up to me.

"Let's wait here a minute," I said as I stood up.

"Why?" Ralph pulled his hands out of his pockets and hung them at his side.

"I'll tell you when we get home."

Back at the house, I decided to take a chance Ralph would sober up enough to understand I needed his help. "Can you come in for a minute?" I nodded at my door. "I need to talk to you about something."

"Sure." He followed me in.

"Coffee?" I held my hand out for him to take a seat on the sofa.

"Nah." He sat down.

I moved a chair over and sat down across from him.

Mr. Bumbles and Alice, who had both been sleeping soundly, awakened enough to fill out the foursome. Alice leapt onto the couch and flipped over for Ralph to rub her belly. Mr. B trotted over and turned his sad eyes up at him, waiting for his turn for some attention. The way they had both taken to Ralph did a lot to mend any negative feelings I had for my cousin. He may have still been playing the part of a twenty-something long after those candles were snuffed out, but he was a decent guy.

"What's up?" He reached down to scratch Mr. B behind the ears.

Hesitating, I debated whether to tell Ralph the whole story, then thought the better of it. If Cobo was as bad as Malachi said, it was best to keep Ralph out of it as much as possible. I rested my arms on my legs and leaned toward him. "Listen, I have a strong sense I'm being stalked. It's probably just me being paranoid, but I wondered if you would be willing to keep your phone on and next to you at night, you know, just in case it *is* something."

"Sure, I don't usually turn it off anyway. This been goin' on awhile? You shoulda told me before."

"It's only been the last few days, but it's made me nervous. If you see anybody out front or on the block that looks like they're up to something, I mean if you sense that something isn't right about them, would you let me know."

"Sure. I got good instincts for that kinda stuff. I can sniff out bums like that." He snapped his fingers, but there wasn't any sound.

"I appreciate it, and I appreciate your including me in on your social life. It would've been lonely moving here without knowing anyone." As judgmental as I had been about him and his friends at times, I meant it. New York was one of those paradoxical places where you could feel isolated among millions.

CHAPTER NINE

Sitting down in my workstation to prepare for my meeting with my boss Collette, I pulled out my purse mirror to double check that the makeup I applied was doing its job. Penny's handiwork had definitely subsided, but I didn't want Collette looking down at me over the top of her too-perfect nose like I was some sideshow freak. As I was tucking my purse away, I realized that despite the reach of Collette's inflated ego I was happy to be there. With the menacing presence of Cobo lingering in the back of my mind, the publishing house was a safe and welcome harbor away from the Bronx.

I was well into my work when I heard the sound of sobbing coming toward me. Poking my head out of the cubicle, I saw Holly standing with her face hidden by her hands and hair. That couldn't be good.

"What happened?" I followed her into her cubicle.

"She fired me," she said between sobs, pulling the pins out of the cat photos that were attached to the wall, and letting them fall to her desk.

"Didn't finish the assignment, huh?"

"No." Pulling open her top desk drawer, she grabbed the contents in her fists and dumped them on top of the cat photos.

Oh boy. "Here, let me help you with that." I stopped her as she went for the next drawer. "I'll find a box."

Without responding, she plopped down on her chair and dropped her hands in her lap.

Returning with two empty banker's boxes from the supply room, I set them on the floor and started loading her stuff into them. She remained in her chair, offering only vague responses when I asked about what items she wanted to take.

It took quite awhile. The woman was a definite hoarder. By the time I was through, the boxes had become too heavy for one person to carry. Darn. Another trip to Cat Hell for me.

"You check around your cubicle for anything we may have missed while I meet with Collette, okay? And then I'll help you home with these boxes."

She sniffled and nodded, her face now splotchy from rubbing her tears.

Taking the *short* chair on the other side of Collette's desk, I perched at the end of it to maintain an equal level with her.

"Your work has been competent and prompt," she said, after a quick hello nod. "So much so that as of today you have moved beyond your trial period."

"Thank you."

"And, since we find ourselves a copy editor short, you can have all the work you think you can handle."

I didn't think another thank you was appropriate, since the offer came at the expense of Holly's livelihood, so I said, "Didn't want to give her another chance?"

"No." She picked up a pile of papers on her desk and tapped them against it, dismissing the topic.

Understanding enough about the legalities of terminating an employee, I knew that was all I was going to get out of Collette regarding Holly, so I dropped the subject. Besides, with little to go on other than she was a cat freak, I had no basis to defend her.

"You've given me plenty to keep me busy for a while, but I have a lot of time to devote to work right now, so if I finish before my deadline, I'll let you know."

"No social life?" She tapped the papers on her desk again, with a mock expression of concern.

Wow. You *are* a bitch. "I've only been in New York a few weeks," I said, defensively enough to let her know she got to me. Damn.

"Well, good luck with that." She turned to her computer.

Staring at her profile, I held my tongue. I needed the job. Had I not, I'd have given her an earful–several hours from then, when I actually came up with a clever retort. I can always count on my brilliant rhetoric to kick in long after the opportunity to use it has passed.

We managed to make it to Holly's place by way of a taxi without her breaking back into sobs. On the ride, she convinced herself that because she was doing such noble work for the cats the universe would provide her with the means to support them. I wasn't so sure.

Struggling under the weight of my box and panting from our walk up the four flights of stairs, I followed Holly down the hallway. When we passed the apartment two down from hers, an old man wearing a tan jacket and reeking of cigarette smoke stepped out.

"Hello, Mr. Pitzer." Holly stopped to greet him. "On your way out?"

"Yup. My niece in Long Island invited me for an afternoon visit and dinner."

"How nice for you." Holly pressed her lips together in a half smile. "Have a great time."

"Will do." He walked off, pulling a cigarette pack from his jacket pocket.

Upon entering her apartment, Holly marched straight through to the kitchen and set her box on the table. "I just knew this day would get better!" She slapped her hands together, almost giddy.

Okay? What turned that around? "I'm glad you're feeling better." I set my box down and kept my eyes away from the kitchen, hoping to avoid seeing Mama Kitty. I assumed she was still alive, since Holly hadn't descended into a deep depression. My previous glimpse of *Mama* had cast her in a recurring role in my nightmares.

"I finally have my chance to save Groucho." She pulled open several kitchen drawers until she found a short metal rod.

"Groucho?"

"Yes. Mr. Pitzer's cat. He's killing him."

"He is?"

"Yes, he's been exposing Groucho to secondhand smoke for years. If I don't get him out of there, he's going to die for sure." She tapped the metal rod against her palm, and started toward her door.

"Wait, where are you going?"

"To get Groucho." She frowned at me like I hadn't been listening.

"But, you can't just go into his apartment and steal his cat."

"Sure I can."

"Won't Mr. Pitzer suspect that you took him, with your interest in cats?"

"I thought of that." She tapped the metal rod to her chin. "And I decided to take him to another cat rescuer. That way Mr. Pitzer will never be able to harm Groucho again."

Oh boy. This is ridiculous! I stared at the back of her crazy head as she rushed toward Mr. Pitzer's apartment.

Squatting down when she reached his door, she turned the knob. "Locked, of course, but I think if I can get this rod in here, and turn it, it will open. I've been practicing." She started working at the lock.

Giving sanity one last shot, I bent over and whispered loudly, directly into her ear, "Holly, this is burglary. You can go to jail for it."

"Sometimes doing the right thing takes great personal risk. I have no fear of the consequences," she said without turning around.

Well, I do! And, she wasn't going to suck me in with her self-sacrificing crap. "I'm not going to be a part of this. I'm leaving." My adrenaline was pumping fast with the thought of being arrested for aiding Holly's criminal activity.

As I took a step toward the stairway, Mr. Pitzer suddenly came rushing at us. "Caught you! I knew you'd been trying to break into my apartment, you thief!" he yelled so loud that the neighbor across the hall cracked her door open and peeked out.

"Cat killer!" Holly yelled back at him, standing up.

"I haven't killed my cat!" Mr. Pitzer grabbed Holly by the upper arm.

"Not yet, but your smoking's going to!" She tried to twist out of his grasp, but he was strong for an old guy.

"The last time I checked, smoking is still legal in this country, but burglary isn't. I've called the cops. They should be here any time. And, you're going to stay right here until they get here."

That was my exit signal. Holding my purse tight to my side, I started for the stairs in a major hurry.

"Mrs. C., stop her!" Mr. Pitzer called to the neighbor. "She's getting away."

Looking back down the corridor, I picked up my speed. The neighbor, whose purple-flowered sweater stretched over arms the size of hams, was chasing me!

She wouldn't have caught up with me, except I ran straight into a New York City police officer just as he crested the last step. When I stopped short, Mrs. C. barreled into me, and we all would have toppled down the stairs, if not for the cop's strong build and steady balance.

"Down here," Mr. Pitzer called to him still holding on to Holly.

Thinking it best not to continue on my flight out of there at that juncture, I walked back down the hall with Mrs. C. and the cop.

"Arrest this thief!" Mr. Pitzer said his chest puffed out like he'd nabbed a felon.

"Arrest this killer!" Holly joined in. "And, make him let me go. He's hurting me."

"Sir, release the lady," the cop said.

"But, she's a thief!"

"And, he's a cat killer!" Holly spat.

"A cat killer?" A crack appeared in the cop's practiced neutral expression. "This man killed a cat?"

"Well, not yet, but he's going to." Holly finally managed to jerk her arm out of Mr. Pitzer's grip. "Secondhand smoke."

"Secondhand smoke?"

"Yes, secondhand smoke. It's as dangerous to animals as it is to humans. More so with cats, because they're so small."

"Smoking is not illegal, but burglary is. Now arrest her," Mr. Pitzer demanded, getting right in the cop's face.

"Sir." The cop took a step back, doing a fine job of maintaining his cool, considering the nut jobs he was dealing with. "Why don't you tell me what happened."

"These two were breaking into my apartment." Mr. Pitzer nodded from Holly to me.

"Now, wait a minute. I had nothing to do with this." I scowled at him.

"Tell him, Mrs. C.," said Mr. Pitzer. All eyes turned to the neighbor lady, who had been standing quietly, her face arranged in a sour expression, her purple ham arms crossed.

"That's right. I seen Holly working at Mr. P's door, and that one helping her." She turned her lemon puss on me.

"I was not helping her." I glared at the woman. "I was trying to stop her. Tell them, Holly." I turned to her.

"That's right. The work to save these helpless animals is all my own." She sighed.

Oh brother. What a martyr! I couldn't believe she had sucked me into helping her.

"So, ma'am, you're admitting you attempted to break into this man's apartment?" the cop asked.

"Yes." Holly nodded.

As he looked from Holly to Mr. Pitzer and back again, he must have been contemplating all the paperwork that would be required if he hauled them into his precinct over a cat issue. Not to mention the ribbing the other officers would give him. "Are you fond of your cat, sir?" he asked Mr. Pitzer, using the same weighty tone he would have on a person of interest in a felony.

"Well, yeah. He's all right. He was really my wife's cat. Been with me a long time."

"Cost you a lot in cat food and vet bills?"

"Food, yeah. Vets, I don't really bother with."

"If what she says is true," the cop nodded his chin at Holly, "and with an old cat like yours, you may not have a choice about those vet bills. You want to be spending your social security on a cat, with cigarettes being as expensive as they are?" He was stabbing in the dark, but doing a fine job of leading Mr. Pitzer where he wanted him to go. Impressive.

Mr. Pitzer scratched his head. "I don't know."

"This lady here seems really concerned about the cat."

"I am," Holly piped up.

"Concerned enough to be willing to pay for his food and vet bills?" He directed a serious stare at Holly.

"Sure, that is, if the cat's with me."

"Now, wait a minute." Mr. Pitzer wasn't going to be led down that road without a struggle. There was his dignity to save. "Are you suggesting I give Groucho to a thief?"

"Mam, do you make it a practice of stealing from people?"

"Of course not. I'm not a thief. I was only trying to save his cat from an agonizing death."

She sure could pour it on. I was thankful I hadn't chosen police work as a profession. I had no clue how they had the patience for the general public.

"And, will you let Mr. Pitzer visit his cat if you take him in? Will you pay for his keep?"

Holly hesitated on that one, casting her eyes up at the ceiling. I knew she was visualizing the throng of cats in her apartment and wondering how she'd be able to take Mr. Pitzer's cat in, and keep *him* out. She didn't want to give him another reason to call the police, and he would likely do so if he found out how far out of code she was on pets per apartment. "Sure," she finally said. It sounded like she was going to let the *universe* deal with that problem too.

"What do you say, sir?" The cop stared hard at Mr. Pitzer. "You're not going to get any other offers to take in an old cat. They're a dime a dozen."

Holly sucked in her breath, looking ready to pounce on the cop for insulting her precious felines. One look from the cop, and she clamped her mouth shut. I guess she had just enough of a toehold in the real world to realize she was getting off easy.

"Well." Mr. Pitzer patted his jacket pocket, checking on his cigarettes again. "I suppose she could have him."

"Really? Thank you, Mr. Pitzer," Holly said. "You're doing the right thing."

"Settled then?" The cop looked from Holly to Mr. Pitzer.

"I guess," said Mr. Pitzer.

"Yes," Holly said with Christmas morning glee.

"Okay for me to go?" I asked the cop, watching Holly swoop in on Mr. Pitzer, chattering away about Groucho.

"Sure."

"I don't really even know these people," I said quietly to him, wanting to separate myself from them. It mattered to me that the cop didn't think I was part of their bag of fruit loops. "Just another one of my good deeds *punished*."

The cop let a little light into his eyes as he absorbed my last comment. "Bye, ma'am."

"Bye."

CHAPTER TEN

Happy to have arrived home before dark the night before, I intended to lock myself in my basement the entire day and throughout the evening. The only exceptions would be pee break for Mr. Bumbles. My plan was to stay as far off Cobo's radar as possible. If cork shoes and cowboy boots appeared in my transom windows I wouldn't know. The blinds were drawn tight.

Deciding that one long midday walk would be the best strategy, because most evil creatures were nocturnal, I followed the jingle of Mr. B's tags into the park a little before lunchtime. The fire hues of autumn that had been licking at the trees the past few days had suddenly exploded, and it was magnificent. We had our beaches and our sunshine, our big valleys and bigger mountains in Southern California, but we only had a hint of fall, an absence I felt every October, all the way down to my DNA, as an arrhythmia in life's heartbeat.

But not that fall. Taking a deep breath, I watched Mr. B follow his nose from bush to bush. The splendor of autumn was far more than crunching leaves and crisp air. It was the promise of a world wrapped in flannel and warmed by a hearth–a realm with time enough for reflection and restoration. There is much to be said for the optimism conveyed by shade-less sun and doing, but the yin to that yang is the peace conveyed by slanted rays, shorter days, and being.

As we moved deeper into the park, I realized we were near the area where I had seen Brandon once before. Not wanting to take any chances, I veered away from it and onto a path I hadn't explored. Lost in thought about my crazy day with Holly, and wondering if she was going to be able to keep Mr. Pitzer away from her apartment, I hadn't noticed that we reached a clearing with a playground. The amount of equipment for children in New York's parks was commendable. This one was empty, however, probably a combination of cool weather, and school schedules.

Wondering if I should continue on around the playground or turn back, I looked down at Mr. B, who had taken the opportunity to sit and scratch behind his ear. When he dropped his paw and the noise from his tags subsided, I thought I heard rustling from behind the bushes on the other side of the playground. Thinking it must be a bird, I started to head back the way I came.

But then I heard the rustling again, this time accompanied by a thud and a moan. What was that? I looked down at Mr. B to see if he had heard it too, conflicted about whether to check it out. Rolling his hound dog eyes up at me, he offered no opinion as to what we should do.

When I heard the moan again, I pulled on Mr. B's leash so he was tight beside me, and crossed the playground. Noticing a path through the bushes to my left, I stepped into it, with Mr. B just behind me. When we had gone a few paces, I saw flashes of movement and stopped.

"Don't. You're going to kill him," I heard someone whisper loudly.

I cringed. The voice sounded familiar. Backing up, I turned to hightail it out of there. Then there was another thud and another moan. "Stop. Stop," the plea was louder and more desperate.

A voice responded in a low but vehement whisper. The only word I could make out was *rock*. *Rock* again? Shit. It had to be Cobo and Brandon, but who was with them? Pulling back almost to the playground, I knelt down and put my arm around Mr. B, unsure if it would be better to hide or run.

I didn't have to decide, thank God, for just then I heard a new voice shout, "Hey, what's going on here?" followed by the sound of heavy footsteps running away.

Standing up, I rushed down the path to where it widened and was intersected by another path, and came across a lunchtime jogger bending over a man who wasn't moving. "Is he alive?" I asked, hooking Mr. B's leash to a low branch and hurrying over and bending down beside the jogger.

"Yeah, barely."

"I'll call 911." I pulled my phone from my pocket.

"Already did, the second I saw those gangbangers wailing on this guy." He showed me the phone he had in his hand.

"Did you get a good look at them?"

"Not really. They ran off fast. Just a young one in a Yankees cap and one a little older wearing cowboy boots. He was the one kicking the life out of him." He looked down at the man.

Noticing the stained twill pants, I realized he was the same homeless man Brandon was with the other day. He was probably behind in paying for his drugs. My stomach heaved at the sight of the bruises forming on his face. "Sadistic bastard," I said, hoping the police and paramedics would get there soon. No one deserved to be treated like that.

"Best not to touch him," the man said when I reached out to put my hand on his shoulder. "You don't know where the injuries may be."

"True." I pulled my hand back. I was better off leaving before the police arrived anyway. It wouldn't be a good idea to share what I knew with anyone other than Malachi. "I'm going to have to leave. I didn't really see anything, and I have to get to work," I lied.

"Okay." The jogger didn't seem too bothered. Holding his cellphone out with both hands, he started taking pictures of the man.

Really? Was nothing sacred anymore? Shaking my head, I walked over to Mr. B.

Keeping my head on a swivel as I walked home, more fearful than ever of being spotted by Cobo, I was thankful they at least hadn't seen me in the park. That would have sealed my fate for sure. I wondered if human trafficking gangs used the same tried and true methods of extermination as the mafia. I really wouldn't want to find myself sinking to the bottom of the Hudson River in cement boots.

I decided to check in with Dori before I called Malachi. Even though she was several years younger than me, her experience and her attitude had aged her in wise ways that I found both enlightening and reassuring. Funny how I still had several girlfriends in Los Angeles, but the last thing I felt I could talk to them about was issues like human trafficking and polygamy. The few times I broached a subject that anywhere near touched on the darker side of human experience, I was shut down by uncomfortable silence followed by a change in topic. I didn't push it. They had a lot of good qualities, but there were times when after I said good-bye to them I felt like we had talked about *nothing.*

Dori had just finished a shift at the restaurant when I called. I gave her a brief rundown on all that had happened since we last talked.

"I told you it was human trafficking," she said, "and I bet Malachi is in the FBI or something."

"Why do you suppose they keep saying the word *rock*?"

"I don't know. It could be a drug reference, or the name of their organization. Have you run it by Malachi?"

"No. I've been so focused on Cobo and his *slaves*, which is so sickening, that I keep forgetting to bring it up."

"Well, you need to tell him and the guy at the anti-trafficking office. I bet one or the other of them will know what it means."

"I'm going to try and get a hold of Malachi to let him know what happened in the park. He said I should only call in case of emergency, but he needs to know this, right?" I wanted reassurance because I felt intimidated by the man, with good reason.

"Definitely."

"I'll stop by the anti-trafficking office too." Shifting on the couch so my legs stretched out and off the end of it, I changed the subject, seeking some normalcy, "So, how's everything going with you? Luke doing okay?"

"Yeah, he's great."

"And you, you still happy about the move now that you've been dealing with L.A.'s manic environment for a few weeks?"

"Sure. It's not perfect. Money's tight, but it's always tight. I'm loving my time at the women's shelter. The people there are amazing, doing great work."

"*You* were doing great work in Harmony, helping Ruthie and other women get away from bastards like Samuel."

Dori had dedicated a lot of her young life to helping women and children escape from Samuel Vaullie, the deranged head of a polygamist compound located just outside of Harmony, and other polygamists like him. She and her group had succeeded in saving one of his underage wives, Ruthie, and her infant daughter from near death through a botched delivery.

"I know, but I was suffocating there."

"I get that. Have you talked to anyone in Harmony lately?"

"Sure."

"Any word on Samuel, speaking of him?"

"Nope. Disappeared into the wind."

"Someone's bound to see him somewhere," I said as Alice jumped up and helped herself to my lap. "He's such a sicko that he's probably plotting to form another polygamist cult as we speak."

"I don't think the rest of the world cares enough about polygamy victims to keep looking for him."

"Really? He's responsible for the deaths of two young women, Dori. He's a murderer."

"The fate of those women is still a low priority for the authorities, like the women I work with here. It's hard to persuade people to get their noses out of their cellphones long enough to see any other needs besides their own."

"Wow. That's cynical. You sound defeated."

"Nope, not at all. Just realistic. The good news is that people like the ones I've gotten to know at the shelter are powerful, take-no-shit types. They'll win in the end. It just may take a while."

I hoped she was right. "How 'bout other news from Harmony? Anything else going on?"

"What else could possibly be going on there, oh, unless you're wondering about Noah?"

"No," I said too quickly.

"Missing him, huh?"

"I didn't say that."

"Sure you are. Why wouldn't you be? You left a hottie behind in that one. Just sayin'."

"Okay. That's enough." I stroked Alice's back. She responded by revving up her purr motor.

"You dating yet, then?"

"I've only been here a few weeks, so, no. How 'bout you. Are you dating?"

"Too busy, but I'll get around to it, and so should you if you're determined to forget Noah."

"I will, but it doesn't happen overnight."

"Oh really? You were in Harmony *one week*."

She was right, but I didn't want to talk about how fast things moved with Noah. "The next time you're at the shelter, why don't you ask that woman you told me about if she has ever heard the word *rock* used in terms of trafficking." I changed the subject.

"Sure, I can do that."

"Let's talk again soon."

"No problemo."

Malachi had no issues with me calling him. He was definitely interested in what happened in the park, as well as my conversation with Martin Moran. When I mentioned I had heard Cobo and Brandon repeatedly use the word *rock*, he didn't comment at all, which made me even more suspicious that there was something to it. As we were hanging up, he again warned me to stay completely away from them. No worries there.

On Friday morning, as I walked through the streets of Midtown Manhattan, enjoying the sunlight and activity, even the sirens, I was hopeful that Malachi was very good at his job. Being confined within the walls of Ralph's basement apartment was going to get old very fast.

After a quick meeting with Collette at the office, where she had to be impressed with my output–ah, the benefits of no life–I decided to head straight over to talk to Vincent.

While I stood at the counter of his office, I noticed him bent over a desk in conversation with a young woman whose hair was plaited and hung over one shoulder. He raised his head and glanced my way when she stopped talking. The earnest expression in Vincent's dark eyes, which were partially obscured by bangs that hung over his glasses, revealed a man who believed passionately in his work. I didn't have to see his apartment to know there were stacks of unopened mail, dirty laundry, and dishes everywhere. Is it the minutiae ignorers of the world who move human progress forward? Unfortunately, I wasn't one of them. Minutiae is my middle name.

He raised one finger to indicate he would be a moment. I took that time to shuffle through the same disorderly stack of literature on the counter I had looked at on my previous time there. Seeing the faces of the victims in the booklets, I was more drawn in by them than I had been before. Oppression of innocent people is an insidious problem, and it was right there in New York and Los Angeles, everywhere, and I had hardly ever heard anyone talk about it before the last few weeks. Had I been living under a rock?

"Sydney." I stuck my hand out when Vincent finally walked over.

"Yes. I remember." He shook it and then put both hands on the counter. "What can I help you with?"

"Some things have happened since we last talked. May I have a few minutes of your time to run them by you?"

"Sure." He walked around the counter and pointed at the chairs we had used before.

After we sat down, I said, "I'm fairly certain now that those people I told you about last time are being trafficked."

"Did you report it to the police?" He straightened his glasses on his nose.

"There are people in law enforcement keeping an eye on the house." I didn't want to reveal anything specific about Malachi.

"How do you know that?"

"I ran into one of them the other night in my cousin's backyard."

"Well, that's interesting."

"It was a brief encounter," I lied, thinking about my scuffle with Malachi in the cellar. "And the officer or whatever he is didn't want to tell me much. I got that, but I do have some questions you may be able to answer."

"I'm not too sure about that."

"I overheard a couple of conversations between a young man and one of the suspected traffickers," I ploughed on, despite his doubt, "and they used the word *rock* more than once. Does that mean anything to you?"

Hesitating and concentrating on the ground, when he lifted his head, he said, "Yeah, it does. Rock is the purported head of a trafficking ring with, we believe, tentacles that reach across the States and around the world. We learned of him from a victim who had the misfortune to challenge him. According to that victim, Rock gets a great deal of perverse pleasure out of personally dealing with laborers who dare to speak up. He brutally beat this victim, and the only reason he survived was because they left him alone, thinking he was unconscious. He was able to escape and use the cover of night to run. A woman in Queens found him collapsed in her backyard, and called the police."

"It sounds like this Rock is right here somewhere in the New York area. Was that victim able to describe him to you?"

"No. He used a blindfold on him. Coward."

"I don't understand why the victims don't escape more often," I said, after sitting quietly long enough to digest the depths of cruelty to which a man can sink. "When I saw them, they were on their own coming home from what I assumed was work. It looked to me like they could walk away anytime."

"And go where?"

"Here, for one thing. I thought that's what your organization's about."

"It's not that easy. I think I told you before they don't have passports, or if they do, the traffickers take them from them. If they're illegal, they don't want to be deported. The hope that they will make enough money to help their families back home is what drives this felonious system. That, and fear of hunger and repressive governments and civil wars, where rape and genocide are the weapons of choice. Even Rock probably doesn't seem as bad to them as what they left."

"So, you're not able to help many of them?"

"Don't get me wrong. It's not a lost cause, or I wouldn't be here." He ran his fingers through his hair. "But, we're fighting for them on a lot of fronts. We have a public relations problem with the segment of the American public who just wants them out of here."

"Oh, boy. There are not a lot of issues in this country more contentious than immigration. So, is it always your goal to keep them here?"

"No, not at all. Most of the time, it's not even possible. Our mission is to treat them with the dignity every human being deserves. We help them navigate our complicated legal system and, in the best-case scenario, we find a family member or sponsor, here or abroad, willing to be responsible for them."

"That's quite an order."

"Yes, but those of us working on human trafficking issues have to keep at it. They're not going away anytime soon, either here or abroad. It's too lucrative." He turned to face me straight on. "You want to help?"

That again? He caught me off guard. Not allowing my eyes to turn from his, I read my instincts, and surprisingly, they said, "Yes. Yes, I do."

"Good. Okay." He nodded.

"You said before you could use help on your newsletter, public relations type things. That would be all I could do for you right now, and I'd need to work mostly from home. Do you have a problem with that?"

"No. Fine by me. No sense wasting time and money commuting."

"Okay, then." I stood up.

He stood also, smiling a half smile for the first time. "What changed your mind?"

"I don't know. Maybe I'm just tired of sitting in the grandstands watching other people fight the good fight. It's time for me to get in the game."

After spending another forty-five minutes going over mailers and the website with Vincent, I wondered why I didn't have more misgivings about agreeing to work with his organization. My norm was to say *yes* solely out of guilt, then to languish in regret. Walking out of the office, I instead was pumped with energy. How about that? I couldn't wait to tell Dori.

CHAPTER ELEVEN

It was Malachi night again at the pub, only it had taken on a whole different meaning than the previous Friday night. There was no way I was going to be able to listen to him sing without thinking how absurd it was in relation to his real life.

I was relieved when Ralph asked if I wanted to walk with him to the bar, because I didn't want to make my way through the dark streets by myself. When we arrived, the place was already throbbing with pheromones and ale. As we made our way back to the table, I kept a lookout for Malachi. My objective for the evening was to get him alone for a few minutes. I had no doubt he knew about *Rock*. If he was as dangerous as Vincent said, I wanted to know how risky it was for me to stay in the neighborhood with the chance that Cobo may have told him about me. The fear that had been gently tiptoeing up my spine had started a cleat-footed sprint.

Greeting Penny, Leeza and Courtney, I noted that Courtney's objective for the evening also must have been to get Malachi alone, but for far more than a few minutes. I hoped that she hadn't paid much for her dress, because it couldn't have been made out of more than a yard of black spandex fabric. It rose so high up her thighs I was hoping that she had remembered her underwear. Otherwise there was going to be way too much sharing going on with the pub patrons.

After giving Penny a quick peck, Ralph walked around the table and pulled a chair up next to Andy and Jared. So many sporting events converged that weekend it was going to take them hours just to figure out what to watch when. On our walk over, Ralph had treated me to a Bubba Gump shrimp-type list of all the different sports, and I tried to act interested, but NASCAR, really? This was New York, not Talladega.

After offering to fetch drinks for the women, I wedged myself between two men standing at the end of the bar and waited for the bartender's attention. She had just noticed me and started my way when Carrick, the pub owner, put his hand on her forearm and stopped her. After saying something into her ear, he came over instead. "Ah, Sydney darlin', where you been keepin' yourself? We missed ya." His bright blue eyes glimmered.

"It's only been a few days since I was last here. You didn't have time to miss me." I smiled.

"Oh, but you bring the flames of the fireside on a misty Irish day with ya, to be sure."

"My red hair again?" I reflexively reached for my head.

"Can't help our yearnin' for our home and our mamos, love."

"I suppose not." I actually was yearning surprisingly little for California. But then, it'd only been a short time.

While I was waiting for my drink order, I turned my back to the bar and took in the room. Watching the relaxed posture of people relieved from their weekday burdens, I was struck by the universality of the human need for a place where the road rises up to meet all that enter. Was this my place? No. Not yet.

"There you go, darlin'," I heard from behind me after a few minutes. I turned to find that Carrick had set my drinks down.

"Thank you." I held out my credit card.

"This round's on the house."

"Oh no, you don't need to do that." I continued to offer the card, feeling uncomfortable at his gesture. He had a business to keep afloat. Why would he be giving his profits away?

"Go on ahead, take the gift." His eyes turned serious.

"Go on," he said a second time, before I could protest again. "You'll be paying me back in time, to be sure."

Okay, that was an odd turn of phrase, especially considering the sparkle had gone from his eyes. Did he think I was a lush who planned on spending most of my paycheck in his pub? No. I was making way too much of what was probably just a kindness. "Well, thank you then, from all of us." I nodded toward our table.

"You be most welcome." Throwing a hand towel over his shoulder, he added, "Malachi will be on shortly, something to light a flame in *your* night, to be sure."

"Well, yes, no. He's a very good singer," I stammered, remembering that Carrick had caught me staring at Malachi the last time. Gathering the drinks, I concentrated on keeping the cool in my cheeks.

"Indeed." He tipped his head. "Go on now, and have a lovely evening. I look forward to our next meeting." He winked.

"Sure, thanks again." I stepped away from the bar.

"Good luck. Good luck Good luck," he said to the rhythm of my steps as I walked away.

What a strange way to say good-bye.

I was not having any luck getting Malachi's attention during his set. The dim lights of the pub made it hard for him to see very far into the audience. When he finally announced he was going to take a quick break, I stood up and moved forward as if I was heading to the restroom. Fortunately, he spotted me and walked my way so our paths would cross. When they did, I said a casual hello, whispered for him to meet me out front in five minutes, and kept moving.

Stepping out the door like I was taking a casual breather, I crossed to the alley side of the pub and away from half a dozen smokers who were chatting softly next to the curb. Malachi emerged from the alley, carrying a pack of cigarettes and a lighter. "Props." He slipped a cigarette out and held it between his fingers. "What's up?"

Whatever works, I guess. I watched him place the cigarette to his lips and flick the lighter. It was bizarre to have him morph from happy-go-lucky Irish lad to *007,* or whatever he was. "When I asked you about the word *rock* you didn't have anything to say," I jumped right in as we had little time, "but since then I've learned *Rock* is actually the head of a dangerous human trafficking ring. Did you know that?"

"Who have you been talking to?" He avoided the question.

"A man who works with victims of human trafficking."

"I thought I told you to stay out of this." His was not a happy tone.

Too bad. If I was in danger, I needed to know. "Look, Cobo has to suspect something about me, the way he acted.

Would he have reported it to this Rock guy? He sounds like a really scary dude, and I want to know if you think I should find another place to live in a hurry."

"If they think you're a threat, there's no place you *could* go, at least in this area, without them knowing about it." He took a drag on his cigarette. If smoking was a prop, he was a natural.

"Oh, good to hear." My stomach tightened. "So, what am I supposed to do? Do you think they'll come after me?"

"Hard to say, but if you're worried, I'd follow my instincts and leave the area until we get this wrapped up."

"And, how long do you think that'll be?"

"I need to get back inside." He sidestepped another question.

As I was about to ask him if he would mind being a tad more helpful, I noticed movement in the alley behind him. I was pretty sure someone had been standing there, lost in the shadows during our entire conversation. I tried to make out the figure as it disappeared down the alley, but it was too dark. "There was somebody there," I nodded over his shoulder, "listening to us."

"They couldn't have heard us. We've been whispering."

"But they were spying on us."

"Maybe."

"How can you be so casual?" I asked, frustrated by his nonchalant attitude.

"They don't pay me to panic." He pulled his cigarette from between his lips, dropped it on the ground, and rubbed it out with his boot.

"I need to find another place to live." The ghost in the shadows had put me over the top. "At least temporarily. If I give you my number, would you be willing to call and let me know when it's all over?"

"You'll know."

"How?" Jeez. He wasn't going to be any help at all. Or, was it he thought I wanted him to have my number? That'd be pretty conceited. Watching his jaw contract and relax, I thought it wouldn't do to have a secret agent without a heavy dose of confidence. I doubted he'd last very long. But, Malachi had no worry from me that I was interested in him. The last thing my heart could stand was being involved with someone who spent his nights lurking about people's backyards.

"Trust me. You'll know." He turned and walked back down the alley.

"I hope so," I mouthed to his back. "I don't want to spend the rest of my life locked in a room with my dog and cat."

When Malachi finished his set, he joined Courtney at a table where she positioned herself so they could be alone. If it was part of his cover, he didn't seem to mind the duty. I even caught him laughing out loud–definitely not the same Mr. Intenso who tackled me in the cellar. He wasn't going to find the bad guys buried in Courtney's cleavage. Forcing my eyes back to the people at my own table, I watched Ralph nuzzle Penny's neck, and Andy entertain Jared and Leeza with a story that involved a lot of hand gestures and impersonations. They weren't going anywhere soon, but I planned to hang in there. I wanted Ralph's company on the walk home.

An hour later, standing outside the pub as everyone was saying good-bye, I discovered that Ralph was planning to spend the night at Penny's. Even though it was a short distance away, I asked them to drop me off at home. I wasn't taking any chances.

Stepping into the dark basement, I reached for the light switch. Despite my worry about the vicious Rock guy, I was going to have to take Mr. B on a brief pee run. As the room brightened I was surprised he was not in his usual spot sacked out on the floor in the kitchenette. Hearing the jingling of his tags to my left, I said, "Hey, bud ..." Then froze. There on the couch was Cobo, relaxed back into the cushions, with his cowboy hat next to him. Mr. B was nearby, happily lapping up the scratching Cobo was giving his ears. To round out the tranquil scene of domesticity Alice was balled up in the opposite corner of the couch from him in a deep sleep.

Run! My self-defense class instructor screamed in my head. The first few seconds are your best chance to survive the ordeal! Tensing, I turned to switch the light back off and flee.

"No, no, no," Cobo taunted. "Don't do that, puta, unless you want your dog's brains all over your walls."

Glancing back over my shoulder, I saw he had moved his hat aside to reveal the gun in his right hand. He had it pointed at Mr. B's head. Shit!

"Or yours." He turned the gun on me.

With my heart pounding and my arms and legs already shaking, I stood rooted to the floor.

"That's a good puta. Now come over here. Let's talk." He waggled the gun.

Stepping around the couch, I stood in front of him, my purse still over my shoulder and my arms crossed tightly in front of me. I didn't know the exact definition of what he was calling me, but it wasn't the first time I'd heard it, and I knew it was nasty.

"You're so tall, like a giant tree full of red birds. Ha!" He laughed as if he had made a clever joke. Only *clever* this guy was not. I studied his vacant eyes.

"Pull that chair over here." He pointed the gun at the kitchen chair behind me. "Sit, sit."

Once I was seated, Mr. B lumbered over to me, sat down, and leaned his weight into my leg. Taking my eyes off Cobo and wishing he would just *poof* disappear like a bad dream, I ran my fingers over the knot on Mr. B's head, wondering, how are we going to get out of this one, boy?

"What do you want from me?" I decided to take the offense in a feeble show of bravado.

"Cobo thought since you so interested in us, you tell me why."

"What do you mean?"

"You no stupid." He jutted his chin out and rested his gun hand on his knee. "Brandon says you watch his house. You ask his father about him. You right there when he talks to me. Why you stalk him? You one of them cougars?"

"What? No."

"Ha! Had you on that one."

The guy was a real jokester.

"You not a cougar, then what you want from Brandon?"

"Nothing. I don't even know him."

"You lie. What you see, huh? What you know?"

"Nothing."

"Lie to Cobo, you hurt yourself." He squinted one eye, pointed the gun at Alice and pretended to pull the trigger. "Kapow!" He turned his small bright white teeth on me in a creepy smile. "And your cat. Don't make me kill your cat. I like cats."

Looking over at Alice, who had slept through her whole mock murder, I scrambled for something to say that would save my animals, and me.

When I took too long to answer, he sat straight up, planted both feet in front of him and leveled the gun at me. "Time to tell Cobo. I got things to do."

I sized him up as a mean sonofabitch who didn't give a rip about anybody but himself. He wasn't going to let me off easily, if at all, so I decided to offer up the drug pusher angle. If that was all I had on Brandon, Cobo may let it go, I reasoned. It was small potatoes compared to human trafficking. "Okay, you're right." I turned my palms up in my lap. "I've been keeping an eye on Brandon. It looked to me like he was selling drugs. I'm not a narc or anything. I just thought he didn't look like a bad kid, and maybe if somebody intervened he could get some help, stay in school and find a legitimate job."

"So, you an angel, sent by the Blessed Virgin to save Brandon, is that it?"

"No. Of course not." What a jerk this guy was. "I'm somebody who thinks young people deserve a chance to make something of their lives."

"Brandon's doing good." Cobo practically spit the words at me, like I'd touched on a sensitive topic. "He helped his padre get the bank people off their back; saved his house; can buy whatever he wants. He don't need your help."

"But, what kind of future does he have?" I was sorry I let the question slip out. It was ridiculous to be having a philosophical discussion with a thug.

"The future's ahora."

Okay? "Anyway, yes, I think I saw him do some drug deals, but I'm not going to turn him in, so if I leave him alone, can we just forget about it?" With Cobo likely his supplier, my guess was the answer was going to be no, but I was desperate.

"You think I believe you? You think I'm stupid?"

"I won't report Brandon. I mean it."

"Like you didn't tell nobody about what you saw at Brandon's house?"

Shit! My shaking moved to my jaw. I clamped my teeth to try and make it stop, and held my breath knowing what was coming next.

"You not so good at keeping things to yourself. You tell people here what you saw, and in Manhattan, in Los Angeles. Anywhere else? You tell anybody in fucking France?" His voice vibrated with barely controlled anger.

Shit! Shit! Shit! My mind spun. They had to have followed me to Vincent's office. Did they know about Malachi? And Los Angeles? Oh, my God. How could they possibly know I told Dori? Unless they had someone working within the women's shelter. Was Dori in danger?

"Nothin' to say?"

No. There wasn't. I had no defense, and I wasn't sure I was capable of speech anyway.

In one swift move, he stood up, closed the distance between us, gripped my upper arm and squeezed. Bending down, he breathed stale garlic breath over my face. "Say good-bye to your puppy and kitty, puta, you're leaving."

"But, he needs to go out." I managed to keep from retching as I turned away from him and looked down at Mr. Bumbles, who was on all fours and as agitated as I had ever seen him. Bouncing up and down on his front paws, he let out a low woof. He sensed something was wrong, but since he wasn't exactly trained as an attack dog, he wasn't going to be of much help. "To pee," I added, relying on Cobo to be enough of a dog lover to have some sympathy for Mr. B's bladder. I thought if I could just get outside with Mr. B as a diversion, there might be an opportunity to scream for help. *Right.*

"He can shit right here." Cobo squeezed my arm even tighter, and pulled me up off the chair with one hand while pointing his gun at Mr. B with the other. "Unless you want me to shoot him instead."

"No! Leave him alone!" I tucked my purse tight to my side and steadied my stance.

"Let's go!" He dragged me toward the couch, set the gun down, put his hat on his head, then picked the gun back up. "You try anything, I shoot you." He dug the gun into my side, narrowing his black eyes at me. "And, I don't miss."

Wincing from the bruise I felt developing on my arm, I looked over my shoulder at Mr. B as he followed us to the door. "Stay, boy!" I hoped he remembered his puppy school training. I didn't have to use the command a lot, as Mr. B spent most of his days *staying*. "That's a good boy, stay!" I repeated, scared shitless that Cobo would follow through and shoot him. Mr. B turned his sad eyes up at me as we went through the door. I prayed it wasn't the last time I would see them.

CHAPTER TWELVE

Cobo led me around Ralph's house to the backyard and past the spot where I hid when spying on Brandon's place. The fall night air was too cool for windows to be open, and it was far too late for anyone to be out in their garden, so Cobo took little care with the sound our footsteps made as we trudged through the bushes and around trees.

At the foot of Brandon's back stairs, Cobo dug the gun deeper into my back. "Up!"

I climbed quickly, trying to inch my way far enough ahead for him to ease his grip on my arm, which had begun to throb. He kept up with me and didn't let go.

When we reached the landing at the top of the stairs, keeping his gun pointed at me, he released me long enough to reach into his pocket for a small ring of keys. Quickly opening the back door, he shoved me into a dark corridor then pulled the door shut behind him. With the gun still pointed at me, he unlocked the first door to our right and opened it halfway. "In!"

When I started to walk through, he stopped me. "No, momento!"

"What?"

"Purse!" He jerked my purse off my shoulder.

Damn. I rubbed my arm where he had twisted it. I was hoping he would forget about my purse. I contemplated pulling the cellphone out and hiding it in my pants on the walk over, but there hadn't been an opportunity.

"Now in!" He grabbed me again and whispered loudly into my ear, "And don't try nothing, or I kill you!"

Repulsed by the dampness from his breath in my hair and with bile rising in my throat from terror at the certainty that *he would kill me*, I stepped into the room.

Hearing the door shut behind me, and a key turn in the lock, I stood for a few seconds unable to see, trying to get my bearings. From the sound of soft whispers coming from the floor not too far from my feet, I was clearly not alone.

It had to be the trafficked laborers. Now what? "Does anyone speak English?" I spoke into the dark.

No answer.

Staring through the blackness trying to distinguish human forms from objects in the room, I decided there was no way I was going to be able to communicate with these people in the dark. Continuing to hear whispers from every corner, I backed up to the door, sat down, stretched my legs out in front of me and leaned against it. It was going to be a long few hours until dawn. And, of course, I had to pee.

Sensing movement, my eyes flew open. I was shocked that I had fallen asleep. Between fear, grunts, snores, and whispers, it couldn't have been for very long.

Clearing my head, I realized every eye in the room was on me. If we were going to help each other, these first few moments were critical. It was important they understood I wasn't a threat, and I was as knee deep in shit as they were.

"Buenos noches," I tried, softening my face into a smile and hoping I had guessed right about their native language.

One of the young women, sitting cross-legged on a blanket against the far wall, covered her mouth, wrinkled her forehead, and looked at me like I was nuts.

Shoot! Good morning wasn't Buenos noches. Why, why, why had I spent all my time in Spanish class passing notes to my girlfriends instead of listening? "English, anybody?" I lifted my hands, palms up, thinking that perhaps last night they had just been shy.

Every one of them shook their heads.

Oh boy. Time to try something different. Quickly surveying the group, I counted four men and two women, who appeared to range in age from their early twenties to forties.

"Me llamo, Sydney." I pointed to myself. Rolling up my sleeve to expose the bruise that had formed on my arm, I winced as I touched it. "Cobo!" I wanted them to know I was a prisoner just like them, not someone sent to watch them. "Gun!" I made a gun out of my hand and pointed it at myself, then pantomimed being dragged. "Cobo brought me aquí." I looked around the room to see if they understood. If they hadn't, at least they were all still staring. "Y tú?" I asked, holding my hands toward them. There were a few slight nods. Good.

Noticing the erectness of the posture of the oldest looking man, who had streaks of gray at his temples, I decided he was a likely candidate for de facto leader of the group. I focused my next words in his direction. "I need to escape so I can get help." I pantomimed running and holding a phone to my ear. "Escape. Help." I repeated the pantomime.

"No."

"Sí. I have to, or your families will never see you again." I knew they had as much fear of being deported as of Cobo, but had to get through to them. Sitting next to one of the younger men was a glass receptacle filled with what I guessed was not apple cider. The idea that they had so little freedom they were forced to urinate in jars made me sick.

"Cobo, bad." I pointed at my arm again. "No stay aquí." I looked over at the women, knowing it wasn't too much of a leap for the trafficking gang to switch from labor to sex. From the way they were huddled together, their dark eyes weary, I wondered if they hadn't been raped already.

Standing up and feeling like Alice in Wonderland after she took a bite of the mushroom, as I looked down on them, I pointed at the window that was covered with a shabby yellowed blind. "Out there. Go. Escape. Help."

"No," the older man said again, this time more forcefully. He turned his eyes away from mine when I looked at him, occupying himself with digging through a plastic bag he dragged to his lap.

My tactics were not going to work, at least not then. They all followed the lead of the older man and turned their eyes away from me. I'd have to try something else to get through to them, or come up with something on my own. Meanwhile, it had been far too long since the last time I'd been to the bathroom, and I wasn't about to use a jar. "Dónde está el baño?" I asked. That question I knew how to ask in Spanish, and about a dozen other languages.

"En el pasillo." A man closest to the door held his arm out to it.

From his gesture, I understood that the bathroom was down the hall somewhere, so I walked over and rapped on the door, hoping it would be Brandon and not Cobo who came. When I didn't get any response, I rapped harder.

After several minutes of knocking, the handle of the doorknob finally turned and Brandon stepped into the room, keeping the door propped open with one hand.

Running my eyes from the top of his brown mop of hair to his cork feet, I said, "Nice shoes." It was the first time I had seen him without his Yankees hat. I guess it wasn't permanently affixed to his head after all.

"Uh, thanks." He looked down also and raised his toe. When he lifted his light-brown eyes back up, the tough guy persona took over from the insecure teenage boy. "What do you want?" He scowled.

"The bathroom."

"It's not time."

"What?" I scowled back at him.

"No bathroom 'til eight."

"People don't urinate by a time clock. I've got to pee now."

"You can't."

"I can, and I will. Watch me." I lifted my shirt, unbuttoned my jeans, and started to pull the zipper down. Behind me the whispers started up again.

"Okay. Just wait." He combed his fingers through his bangs. "I'll take you there."

Walking by him and waiting while he locked the door behind him, I quickly scanned the hallway trying to understand the house's layout. There was the door we had come through the night before at our end, and a window facing the front at the other end. As I followed Brandon down the hall, we passed a narrow stairway that led to the first floor. Glancing up, I also noticed an attic access with a short frayed rope attached to it.

When we reached the room just beyond the stairway, he opened the door. "This is it."

"What? No key?" I frowned at him as I stepped in.

"I'll be right out here, waiting for you. Make it fast." He crossed his arms and leaned into the wall, his shoulder pushed up against the doorframe.

The room was disgusting. It reeked of urine and worse. The shower stall was covered in mold. The toilet and sink hadn't been cleaned in months. There was no soap, and no toilet paper from what I could see, and my shoes clung to the sticky, faded vinyl floor. *Icky. Icky. Icky.* I shuddered.

I cracked the door open and poked my head out. "How can you make those people live like this?"

He shrugged. "Let's go."

"I haven't peed yet," I said, accusingly. "There's no toilet paper.

"So."

"So. I need some."

"No."

Staring him down, I knew I wasn't going to get anywhere for the moment. I closed the bathroom door and took care of business, making as minimal contact with any surface as possible.

"Your folks couldn't have raised you like this." I glanced over at him as we walked back to the room. No time like the present to start trying to drive a wedge between Cobo and Brandon.

"How do *you know*?" He didn't look back at me.

"I know your dad thinks you're someone to be proud of. So, act like it. You wouldn't treat a dog the way you're treating them." I gestured down the hall. "I get that Cobo calls all the shots, and that you have to be his slave. But what harm would it do if when you're out today you buy some toilet paper and cleaning supplies. It's not like they're going to soap themselves up and slip down the drain."

Watching indignation, then perplexity cross his face, I knew I had gotten to him. "You don't know what you're talking about," was the only response he could muster.

"I do. And, so do you," I said as he unlocked the bedroom door, and I walked back through.

An hour into the morning, I gave up trying to get through to my roommates. They were suspicious of me, and I didn't blame them. I'm sure that a white redhead who spoke crazy Spanish was not exactly their idea of an ally. And, it wasn't like I had hatched some great plan to save us all anyway.

Right on schedule at eight, although I couldn't verify it because I didn't have my cellphone, Brandon began the bathroom rounds. It didn't take long, as he allowed them very little time each. A few came back with wet hair, trying to stay clean with what little was available to them. As soon as the last one returned, Brandon held the door open, and they obediently marched through it and off to forced labor.

It still puzzled me why they hadn't tried to run away. There was so little I understood about conditions in one country, that would make people choose to live as slaves in another. I looked around the room at the thin blankets and torn plastic bags holding everything they owned.

Brandon had avoided eye contact with me on his departure. I took it as a sign of guilt, a good thing if I was going to persuade him away from the dark side.

A few minutes after they left, I lifted the blind and scanned the backyards, wondering if I should force the window open and yell for help. No. It wasn't backyard weather. Brandon would hear me long before anyone else.

Pacing the room, I was desperate to find a way out–soon. I had a much better chance of escaping with Brandon as guard than Cobo. Riffling through the drawers of the nightstands and dresser, remains of a time when this was a bedroom rather than a prison cell, I searched for anything to help.

There was nothing of use in them, just two sweaters that smelled of musty wool and cigarettes; yellowed tissue paper; several buttons; and a knit beret, its threads frayed and worked loose. Squatting to look into the back of the bottom dresser drawer, I pulled out a framed photograph of a couple holding the hands of a toddler who was standing between them all smiles. Brandon's family portrait. Sad.

What happened? Was it your husband's alcoholism? Did you run away, Mrs. Moran, I wondered, looking at the pretty young woman who stared back at me from the frame. Why didn't you take Brandon with you? Are you still alive?

How do you go from the hope of all things new and good to Martin Moran weaving his way down the street, beers under his arm, and Brandon dealing drugs?

Standing up and placing the framed photo on top of the dresser, my stomach growled, loudly. That was it. I was hungry, a condition that made me really testy. Breakfast had been a large box of donuts Brandon shoved into the room. The one or two questioning looks I received when I glanced over at the box told me that the trafficking victims were not getting enough to sustain them through their days. I didn't take one.

My patience gone, I pounded on the door. When I didn't hear anyone coming, I pounded again, knowing Brandon had to be close by, as he probably had strict orders from Cobo to stand guard over me.

Finally opening the door, he said, "Yeah?" then tipped his head and tossed the bangs from his eyes. He was dressed in the same thick, hooded sweatshirt I had seen him in earlier, even though the house had warmed up.

"I need to eat."

"You had breakfast."

"Noooo." I scowled at him. "*They* had donuts, which is not good for them at all. Cobo and his gang are lousy businessmen if they think they're going to make any money off malnourished laborers."

"Huh?" Brandon didn't follow that at all.

"Look. I'm hungry. I'm thirsty. I need you to go down into your kitchen, scrounge me up something to eat and bring it back here. Or, I'll go down there with you and do it myself."

Hesitating like he really had to think about it, he finally mumbled, "No. I'll do it," and shut the door.

When he returned, he was carrying a lopsided peanut butter and jelly sandwich on white bread, and a glass of water. I tried to ignore the smears on the glass. I didn't want to think about what microscopic bugs could be crawling around on it. "Thanks." I took the plate and glass from him. "I need you to hang around until after I eat to let me use the bathroom."

"I'll wait out here."

"Why don't you come in? I'm bored as hell. It won't hurt to sit here 'til I'm done eating."

He scratched under his chin with his index finger. "Okay, but no funny stuff. I've got a gun." He pulled a small revolver out of his pocket. That's why he was wearing the sweatshirt.

"Fine." I tried to act calm. I had zero trust in a sixteen-year-old's ability to handle a gun. With Cobo, any gun use would be deliberate. With Brandon, there was a big risk of an accident.

"You into the Yankees?" I asked, sitting down crossed-legged on the floor, planning to keep the conversation light, at least for starters.

"Yeah." He leaned against the wall.

"Ever go to a game?"

"Box seats." He tried to act casual about it, but from the excitement in his eyes, it was a big deal to him.

"Really? That's fun. Whose box?"

"A friend of Cobo's."

"Hmm." I took a bite of the sandwich, and followed it up with a swig of water. "These friends of Cobo's, how do you think they afford that box? Drug money? Trafficking money?"

"I don't ask." He dug his hands into his pockets.

"You may want to, Brandon, because the deeper you get in with this gang of Cobo's, the less likely it is you're going to see freedom until you're a very old man."

"Shut up." He leaned forward from the wall.

"Think about it, Brandon. Drug dealing is going to get you prison time enough, but add to that human trafficking, kidnapping."

"We never kidnapped nobody."

"Yes, you did. Me. And, what do you think trafficking is? Those are all felonies, Brandon, with years in prison attached to each one of them. They will try you as an adult, and your dad will be long dead before you ever get out of prison, with all the crimes you're racking up."

"Shut up," he repeated. "Just shut up."

"No. You need to hear this. You don't seem like a bad guy. You don't like the way Cobo treats helpless people. It makes you feel sick, right Brandon?"

"I said, shut up!" He stepped over until he was almost on top of me and pulled out his gun, but held it at his side.

"The only way to avoid spending a lifetime in prison," I continued, ignoring the gun, "is to help me get out of here, and come with me to the authorities. I know they'll go easy on you if you cooperate."

"Sure, they'll go easy on me, but do you think Cobo's gang will, huh?" His voice took on a high desperate pitch that belied his youth. "No way. I go to the cops, and I'm dead. I'm dead, and my dad's dead."

"They'll protect you."

"Right. The way they protected my mom?"

"What happened to your mom, Brandon?"

"Nothing. Never mind." He swung the gun in my direction. "Just get up and go to the fucking bathroom, and leave me alone."

"Okay." I set my plate aside, unfolded my legs, and stood up, slowing my breathing and staying an arm's length from Brandon. I had pushed it far enough. I didn't know how I was ever going to help him overcome his fear of being hunted down by Cobo's gang. Maybe he was right. Maybe it was an impossible task to keep him and his father safe. I hoped that

Malachi and his people at least had the opportunity to try. Otherwise, it was probably me who was going to be long dead.

As Brandon stepped aside for me to get to the hallway, he looked over at the dresser and froze. "Where'd that come from?" He stared at the family photo, but didn't reach for it.

"I found it in a drawer."

"Why'd you do that, you nosy bitch?" His voice sounded like that of a desperate teenager, as he once again held the gun up at me. "Put it away. Put it away, now!"

Pulling the top dresser drawer open, I set it on top of the wool sweaters, closed it, and turned to him. "I meant no harm."

"Just get to the fucking bathroom." His voice caught in his throat.

"Okay, fine. I will, Brandon." I lowered my voice to an empathetic tone. No use rattling him anymore. He was a hurting young man, and I had the strong sense things were not going to end well for him.

CHAPTER THIRTEEN

Sorting through my options for escape, I decided that none of them were without the risk of my being caught, and maybe even killed. There was the hope that the lecture I had given Brandon about spending the rest of his life in prison might make him want to stay away from me. There was even the possibility that as an antsy teenager, he would abandon his post and leave the house. Another thing working in my favor was that the slave laborers he had been living with had likely given him the impression that escape was impossible.

And, maybe it was, but I was going to try anyway.

I had come up with two plans to break out of the house. The one involving opening the window and removing the bars, I dismissed right away. Even if I had managed to muscle the bars loose, it was a two-story drop down to a cement landing.

My other plan was to jimmy the lock on the bedroom door, and the one on the back door, then flee down the stairs to the backyard. From there it was a quick jog to Ralph's house.

But, how? I jiggled the doorknob, then squatted down so I was eye level with the lock. I had no idea what I was looking at or looking for. I was just copying what I had seen in the movies. In those movies, didn't they use credit cards to pick locks? No credit cards here. I turned to scan the room. Honing in on the plastic bags belonging to the trafficking victims, I thought there could be something in one of them I could use on the lock. I was uncomfortable going through their meager belongings, but rationalized it by knowing that my freedom, and theirs, depended on it.

Methodically making my way from one blanket to the next, I bent down, picked up a bag, and felt my way through it, searching with my hand rather than eyes, feeling like that was somehow less of a violation. In the first three, I felt only fabric, but in the fourth one, within rolled cloth at the bottom of the bag, I felt something hard. Drawing it out and unwrapping it, I discovered a steak knife, then one in the fifth bag as well. So, they weren't as complacent as they acted. But, was it a defensive or offensive weapon? Were they planning their own escape?

Finding nothing but clothing in the last bag, I took the two knives over to the door, squatted down, and tried sliding a knife tip between the door and jamb several times. Nothing happened. Damn. Maybe it wasn't the kind of lock that could be opened that way. Now what?

Starting to grab the knob in frustration, I noticed a tiny hole in it. Was that how it worked? Maybe if I could find something small enough to stick in there, it would release the lock. But, what? I didn't wear hairpins, and hadn't found any in the bags belonging to the two women.

Looking over at the small empty closet that I had dismissed on my several rounds of scavenging for tools, I remembered seeing a lonely wire hanger on the floor.

Hurrying over, I plucked it from the dust and began straightening it.

Kneeling, I slowly inserted the end of the hanger into the lock, careful not to bend it. Pushing and pulling it like a probe, I finally felt the lock give.

My God, it opened! I did it! One down. I turned the knob, cracked the door open, and peeked out, looking toward the stairwell. Trying to calm the rush of blood in my ears, I listened hard for any sound from the first floor. I heard nothing.

Carrying a knife and the hanger, and pulling back on the door slowly to avoid any squeak, I tiptoed the few steps to the back door. Bending down with confidence at my new talent–burglar for hire–I noticed there was no pin hole in that door handle, and set the hanger aside. Pushing the tip of the knife between the door and jamb, it only slid in a quarter of an inch. I didn't know why I was even trying. It was a heavy wood door with a thick deadbolt, locked from the inside and outside. There was no way to break it open.

Nervous about the seconds ticking by, I looked back over my shoulder and up at the hallway ceiling, and honed in on the attic access. Holding my breath, I again listened for sounds from below. Still nothing. So, the attic it was. Tiptoeing back into the bedroom, I returned the knives to their bags, hoping the owners would not have to use them, then I lifted one of the nightstands, carried it down the hall, and positioned it under the attic opening.

Reaching up, I grabbed the short frayed rope and tugged. It didn't budge. Gripping it even tighter, I pulled with every bit of force my puny arms could muster. It gave. Holding it steady, I wondered how I was going to unfold the ladder without being heard.

My only choice was to move fast and pray. Carefully lowering the bottom rungs, as soon as the ladder hit the floor, I rushed the nightstand back into the bedroom, hurried back, and scrambled up, folding the steps up behind me as I ascended. When I reached the top, I scooted into the attic, while controlling the ladder so the springs wouldn't slam it shut.

When I was satisfied the attic door was closed tight, I stood up, and waited for my eyes to adjust to the dim light. They focused fast, as the dormer window that faced the front of the house was covered in a tattered curtain that let in slivers of sunlight. Taking small soft steps, I tiptoed around abandoned furniture and boxes strewn throughout the space, on the lookout for critters. The last thing I needed was to come across a rat, because I was pretty sure I wouldn't be able to keep my shrieks to myself.

When I reached the dormer window, I sighed in relief. It wasn't barred, and if I tightened my ass and sucked in my belly I thought I should be able to squeeze through it. Staring down at the roof that covered the second story, I calculated if I scooted down it, I could then drop to the metal awning that covered the front door and finally to the front porch.

Pushing up on the window latch, it didn't budge. Damn. So much for my sense of relief. It had probably been decades since the last time someone used it. Hammering the frame with my fists didn't help either. Time to put my long legs to good use. Shoving a box under the window that was heavy and strong enough to hold me, I stepped onto it, and after steadying myself, kicked hard at the window frame. It still didn't budge. Undeterred, I kicked again, this time so hard my foot slipped and broke through the pane.

Wildly swinging my arms to keep myself from falling backward, I jerked my foot back through, catching it on a protruding shard of glass. Shit! I watched blood ooze through my sock. Under normal circumstances I would be a big baby about it–blood always made me woozy. But, there was no time now. I had to ignore it.

Pounding my fist on the frame again, I realized it had loosened. Bringing my non-bloody foot up to window level and conscious of keeping it on the frame only, I kicked hard. It finally gave. After opening the window all the way, I pulled the sleeves of my sweater down over my hands to avoid getting cut by the glass that had fallen on the roof, and put my arms through, followed by my head and torso. I slid my hips through with zero room to spare. One more trip to the gelato shop, and I'd have been in deep doo-doo.

After I righted myself, I looked out at the yellow and orange treetops, then down to the sidewalk below. I thought about screaming for help, but was afraid that with as little activity as there was on the street Brandon might be the first one to hear me. I still wasn't sure if he was home or not.

Continuing on my planned route, I scooted down the roof, trying to keep any pressure off my bleeding foot. When I reached the gutter, I swung both legs over, and stared down at the short drop to the metal awning over the front door. The thing didn't look very sturdy, but even if it gave, at least it would break my fall.

Once I hit that awning, I would have to slide down, then dangle my feet over and try to reach the porch rail. When I finally hit the ground, I planned to get out of there fast, because if anyone was still in the house, they were going to hear the commotion and come running. I was fortunate there hadn't been a response to the noise I had already made, but that was two stories up from where I imagined Brandon reluctantly kept guard. The front porch was definitely in earshot.

Gauging the distance between the tip of my toes and the awning, I told myself it wasn't far, so I forced myself to keep my eyes open, scooted to the very edge, and dropped down. On landing, the aluminum posts creaked and swayed, but held. The dent I created was going to take a long time to hammer out, however.

Rolling on to my stomach, I slid down the awning. Fortunately, it was covered in so much dirt and rust, there wasn't a chance I'd slip off. The next stage, however, was a different story. As I slowly inched over the edge, I stretched my legs out, hoping to reach the porch rail before the weight of my body plummeted me to the ground.

I felt the rail with the toes of one foot then the other, and gripping tightly to the edge of the awning, I settled on to my feet. My God! It worked! I'm going to get away!

Once I steadied my swaying, I let go of the awning, bent down, and grabbed the rail, then leapt on to the porch. Shaky, I looked down at my bloody sock. It could have been a whole lot worse.

Looking back up, I stared right into the barrel of a shotgun held by Martin Moran, who had stepped out of the shadow of the awning.

"What the hell you doin'?" he snapped, his eyes slightly unfocused and graying hair pressed to the side of his head.

"Ruining my property, trying to rob the place." He looked up at the awning, the gun vibrating in his shaky hands.

"What? No!" I drew back, wrapping my arms around my torso to try and steady my own shaking. Oh, that was rich. Accuse *me* of robbery. "Do you have any idea what's been going on in *your property?*"

"Sure do. A crazy redhead's been leaping out my window."

Unbelievable. "Yes. Because this crazy redhead was kidnapped and imprisoned in your bedroom along with six other people! Mr. Moran, a dangerous human trafficking gang is operating out of your house, do you understand me?"

"You're nuts, and I'm calling the police."

"Please do. Do you have your phone with you?"

"No." He looked confused.

"Let's go get it." I unwrapped my arms, ignoring the gun, and then thought I had better ask, "Is Brandon in the house?"

"No. He's out."

"Okay, good." I started to move around the barrel of the gun toward him.

"What're you doin'? Get back there." He waggled the gun.

More frustrated than afraid, I said. "You *do know* Brandon's involved in drug dealing, and he's been guarding the slave laborers in your house."

"They're renters." He didn't address Brandon's drug dealing.

He probably liked having him in the business–an income, and the drug supply didn't run out like the beer–revolting. "Have you watched them come and go, Mr. Moran?" I scanned his face for any degree of morality. With his grizzled appearance, he looked old, but was probably not even out of his forties. "Do they look like renters to you?"

"Haven't seen 'em. I bunk in the basement."

"It's still the same house. You haven't seen them?"

"Nah."

This was going nowhere, and I needed to get home and hope that Ralph was there. "You're saying you don't know what's going on doesn't change the fact that Brandon is caught up in some very dangerous stuff. If you want to see him make his next birthday, you may want to start paying better attention. I'm leaving now." I backed away from him and toward the steps, hoping that he was all bluff.

"But you broke into my house," he protested.

"Right, so where's the loot then?" I frowned at his stupidity. "I told you I was kidnapped, and now I'm leaving to call the police."

"But, my awning." He looked up.

Oh my God! How does someone get that pathetic? "Your awning is the least of your worries. I'm leaving." I turned my back on him and descended the steps. I didn't have time to argue with a muddled brain, shotgun or not.

As I turned to glance up the street, I noticed a black-hatted head sauntering toward me. "Shit. Cobo!" His gait wasn't rushed, so he hadn't seen me yet.

Turning to look back at Moran, I ordered, "Go! Now! Find Brandon and disappear, or you're both dead, I promise. And, call the police. I mean it. Don't fool with these people. Tell them what's been going on here. Tell them Cobo is after me. My name's Sydney. Sydney Roberts."

Looking in Cobo's direction, I saw him check up and move faster. He spotted me! I rushed back up the steps, by

Moran, across the porch, and leapt over the rail to the side yard.

Running at full tilt in what had become a familiar path around bushes and trees, I headed for Ralph's house. And I almost made it too, at least I thought I had, before I collapsed to the ground and everything went black.

CHAPTER FOURTEEN

Cognizant of voices barely audible over the hammering in my skull, I kept my eyes closed, trying to recall where I was. I had no idea. As I became more fully conscious, I did know my wrists and ankles were tied to a hard metal chair, and my mouth was taped. Not good.

The pain from the cut on my constricted right foot and the sticky hair on the back of my neck filled in the rest of the blanks. Cobo must have caught up with me, knocked me out, and brought me there. But, where?

I concentrated on keeping my breathing deep and my eyelids quiet to listen to my captors before they realized I was awake. There were three voices. One I recognized as Cobo's. The other two were not familiar. At least Brandon wasn't there. I hoped that meant his father found him and the two of them were out of the traffickers' reach. I don't know why I was worried about them. They hadn't seemed at all concerned about me. It must have been that family photo. I'm a sucker for sad stories, and theirs more than qualified. I also hoped they let the police know about the trafficking victims and me, and that someone was on Cobo's trail.

The voices were not right next to me, more like a few yards away. The way they echoed made me think we were in a large empty space with high ceilings. Their voices were low, but I picked up a word here and there. One of those was *rock*– of course. I might finally find out who he is. And after that I was going to die.

When they used the word rock again, I could hear them better. They were talking like they expected him to show up very soon. Oh boy. Someone named Rock was probably not the warm and fuzzy type.

With my muscles buzzing from being confined in one position and unable to remain completely still any longer, I shifted in my seat, hoping they wouldn't notice. Wrong.

In three swift taps of boot heels across a cement floor, Cobo was right on top of me. "Open your eyes, puta. We know you're in there."

Straightening my head, which was still in so much pain I thought I might be sick, I hesitated. With my eyes closed, it was a nightmare. With them open, it would be a reality far worse.

Without warning, Cobo slapped me hard across the face, jerking my head back and setting fire to my cheek.

Moaning, I dropped my head, feeling the bile crawl up my esophagus.

Grabbing my chin, he lifted it until I was forced to look into his eyes. "When I tell you to do something, you do it, comprende?"

I nodded slightly to let him know I understood. If I was going to survive the next few minutes, I better cooperate. Cobo was clearly without mercy. Rock too, undoubtedly, but I'd like to live long enough to find out.

"Why you want to leave us when we so good to you?" Cobo pinched my chin between his fingers until tears sprung into my eyes. "You think you pretty smart, eh, escaping like James fucking Bond." Glancing over his shoulder, he looked to his two accomplices for validation of his wit. They complied by forcing themselves to laugh.

Following Cobo's glance, I knew immediately I wasn't going to get any sympathy from them. In their early twenties, they were white, and wore short-cropped hair, expensive leather jackets, heavy gold chains, and sneers.

"You not feel so smart now." Cobo twisted my head back and forth, pinching my chin even harder. "What's that you say? No?" He laughed and bent down so that our noses almost touched. "You no going anywhere this time, and when Rock through with you, I finish up. See how you like that." He straightened up and jutted his pelvis at me. "You one lucky puta!" He laughed again and walked over to the two men.

Dropping my head back down, I tried to take deep breaths. My nose wasn't covered, but the tape over my mouth and the panic rising in my chest made me feel like I could suffocate. The chances were very good I had a concussion that should be looked at and a foot that needed stitching. And I was so thirsty. Even if I weren't tied up, my odds for survival were pretty slim.

Glancing up under my hair, which was curling down over my face, I studied my surroundings. From the oily metallic smell and cavernous size, the space at one time must have been a mechanic's shop. There was a pull-up door beyond the three men, with a solid exit door next to it. All of it looked impenetrable.

The men sat on metal chairs like the one I was tied to. From their body language and the tone of their voices, the two younger men seemed to be trying to one-up each other, either that or impress Cobo. I don't know why. Maybe they were looking for a promotion–to private first class in the army of scuzzballs. One of the men's voices had a trace of an Irish accent. If so, maybe we were still in the upper Bronx. I hoped so. Somehow it made me feel better to think that Ralph was nearby, and Malachi even better.

At the sound of the exit door opening, I lifted my head to see Carrick, the pub owner, walk through it, followed by two men who looked a lot like the twenty-something thugs with Cobo.

Carrick? My first response at seeing him was relief, followed immediately by confusion. What is *he* doing here?

Joining Cobo and the other men, the new arrivals bent their heads and spoke in whispers, then after a few minutes, Carrick walked over to me, leaving the others staring after him.

Planting his feet in front of my chair, he reached down, grabbed the corner of the tape that covered my mouth and ripped it off.

Wincing from another assault on my already stinging face, it was pretty clear that Carrick had not come to swoop in and rescue me. Focusing my eyes on the floor, I tried to stay sharp enough to give myself a glimmer of hope of getting out of there alive. I commended my intuition for recognizing during our last few exchanges at the pub that something was not quite right about the guy. For all the good that was going to do me.

"So, red-headed Sydney from California." He grabbed a fistful of my hair and tugged on it. "Who you working for?"

What? No greeting me with how I remind him of his mamo? Funny how his accent wasn't nearly as strong as when he was at the pub.

When I didn't respond right away, he tugged harder, forcing my head back. "Who is it?"

Staring at the hard lines of his muscled chest under his knit black shirt, I wondered if he could be the elusive *Rock*. That would make this happy-go-lucky Irishman the head of a vast and deadly trafficking cartel. Scary. I shivered. Make that super scary. "I'm not working for anyone." My voice was hoarse from dehydration.

"Not a good answer."

"But, it's the truth." I struggled for an even tone, trying not to reveal the heart-pounding panic that gripped me.

"All that sneaking around? You just doing it for fun?"

"No." I decided to buy some time by telling him about my movements over the last two weeks; sure that he already knew what I had been up to anyway. "I'll explain, but I need some water."

He looked over at the men. "Get a water."

One of the lowlifes reached into a backpack that was leaning against a chair leg, pulled out a plastic bottle and brought it over.

Carrick released his hold on my hair and held the bottle up to my lips so I could drink. Quite a bit of the water dribbled down my chin and on to my shirt, which brought goose bumps to my flesh. The building was damp and cold, and my sweater was not helping.

"Okay, tell me your tale." He pulled the water from my mouth, set it on the ground and crossed his arms.

I related my encounters with Brandon and the trafficked laborers, leaving out any references to Malachi or Dori, although I was pretty sure from Cobo's allusion to Los Angeles that they somehow knew she had been talking to me about the trafficking gang.

"That's a pretty story, girl, but none of that tells me why someone who just moved here from California would be lurking about at night, putting herself in the path of the likes of them." He nodded at the men.

"Like I told Cobo, in watching Brandon, it seemed like with help there might be a way to convince him to find something better to do with his life than sell drugs." I clamped my teeth together to quell the chattering that vibrated my jaw.

"So, ya did have help."

"No. No help." I could barely get the words out. "I hadn't thought it through. I just hoped there was a chance for him to turn his life around. You know the rest."

"And you never talked to anyone else about what you saw?"

Knowing he would have to see my eyes if there was a chance of his believing my answer, I looked up into his blue ones, which had long lost their bogus twinkle. "I asked some people in the neighborhood about Brandon, and talked to someone at a non-profit about human trafficking." I was sure from the things Cobo said to me I wasn't giving up anything they didn't already know. It was what I wasn't saying I hoped Carrick couldn't read in my eyes.

Watching his jaw constrict, I knew I hadn't gotten away with anything. Bringing the knuckles of his right hand up to his face, he slowly rubbed them over his chin. Staring hard at me, his eyes turned from neutral to malevolent.

Tightening my muscles against the restraints, I braced myself for what I knew was coming next.

"You think me an eejit, woman, is that it?" He pulled his hand away from his jaw, keeping his fingers curled into a fist.

I shook my head.

"But, you expect me to believe you didn't go to the police."

"I didn't. I wasn't sure about the trafficking until Cobo threw me in a room with the people you have locked in there." I stuck to my lie.

Uncurling his fist, he leaned forward, grabbed my throat, and squeezed.

Wriggling in my chair, I twisted, trying to pull out of his grasp.

He squeezed harder, until I was sucking for air. "And, I suppose you also want me to believe that Malachi is just a pretty boy who can sing."

"Stop!" I rasped, desperate for breath.

Easing up, he kept his hand around my throat.

Taking in several gulps of air, I closed my eyes, feeling like I was on the edge of passing out.

"Tell me what you know about Malachi." He pressed his thumb and middle finger into my bruised skin.

"Don't," I rasped out, panicked at the thought of him closing off my airwaves again. "Okay, I'll tell." How was he on to Malachi? And, if he was, why did he need me? I tried to turn my focus away from the intense fear and pain that wracked my battered body.

"Now!" Carrick yelled down on top of me so loud my ears rang.

"Okay." I trembled so hard the chair was shaking. "Malachi found out somehow I had been checking up on Brandon and approached me. He must be an undercover cop, but he never told me who he works for, or what he's doing. That's the truth." I took a ragged breath.

Finally pulling his hand from my throat, he straightened, his arms hanging relaxed at his side, belying his steely glare. "I believe you, which makes you of no use to me." Without warning, he raised his booted foot and shoved it into my chest, toppling my chair over, and knocking my head onto the cement floor.

Still conscious, but barely, as Carrick's voice and footsteps faded toward the door, I heard him say, "Get rid of her. Let me know when it's done. I need you back with the spics right away, and we need someone to hunt down Brandon."

So, this is it! I wished I could at least reach my hands up to cradle my poor skull. It hadn't housed the most brilliant of brains, but it served me well. And now it's over! This is where my life ends! Before marriage. Before kids. Before making any kind of difference to anyone. A vision of Harmony sprang to mind, of the red rocks, of Dusty's, of Dori, Luke, Cal, V.A., and Noah. Why that vision over all else in my life, I didn't have the mental capacity left to fathom.

I would have cried, except Cobo didn't give me any time. He was standing over the top of me the minute I heard the door close. Pretending to be unconscious, I laid very still, not hard to do, considering I was tied up and out of fight.

Sticking the toe of his boot into my upper arm, he called over to his buddies. "She's out. Get the tarp from the car. It'll be easier to drag her out on it."

"But, I thought you were gonna fuck her, boss, maybe pass her along to us," one of the voices whined. A real gem of a human being.

"You heard Rock. We gotta get back."

Despite his swagger, Cobo wasn't the alpha male in the pack. He answered to Carrick, and tolerated slurs against his own race without comment. There was a coward in him I'd like to challenge, but I wouldn't have the chance. At least it sounded like Brandon was okay. Maybe he even did the right thing and sent the police looking for me. Too late, since I was going to be flat out on a tarp and covered in blood in a few minutes! But, it was a good note to die on–the hope there was a chance for change for the better in everyone. But then, maybe not quite everyone ... I heard Cobo and his buddies rustling around the warehouse, preparing for my murder!

Untying me from the chair, two of the men grabbed me by the arms and legs, and flopped me down on what I assumed was the tarp. I was sore in so many places and was so weak that my lifelessness was not an act. Whatever means they came up with to end my life, I had no plans to witness it. My eyelids were locked shut, and they were going to stay that way.

"Where do you want her?" The man at my head called across the room.

"Slide her over here," Cobo answered, "and then go out and make sure there ain't nobody around to hear the shot."

After I was dragged across the room and I heard one of my captors exit the building, I felt the point of a boot probing my side. "Wake up, puta," Cobo said. "Time to die." I didn't respond.

He dug his boot harder into me, but I held on–my last act of defiance–I wasn't going to break.

"She's out pretty good," Cobo's goon said to him.

"Yeah, and *you* gonna off her."

"Yeah?" He didn't sound very sure of himself.

"You always sayin' you want more to do. This is it."

"But I never offed nobody before. Least ways, you know, not like this."

"You sayin' you don't wanna do it?" Cobo stepped away from my side and moved toward the other voice. "Because, I do it," his voice was low and menacing, "I off you too."

"No, boss, I'm doin' it. I'm doin' it." The man scrambled for words. "I just, you know, need to know what you want, I mean, how you want it done."

"It ain't too hard," Cobo said in a mocking tone. "You put the gun to the side of her head, and kapow, pull the trigger. Think you can do that, dumb shit?"

"Sure, boss."

"Jesus," Cobo used the Spanish pronunciation, his voice turned toward the exit. "How long it fucking take to check around? Go get him," he commanded.

Hearing the door close, I knew it was just Cobo and me now, and I wondered if I could summon the strength to fight him. Not really, but if I was going to die anyway, why not try? Listening for his position in the room, I heard the sound of his toe nervously tapping a few feet away. Opening one eye a crack, I saw him standing, his head turned toward the door, swallowing water from a plastic bottle. Perfect.

Frantically reviewing my options, I knew I only had a few seconds. I hadn't seen any means of escape other than the exit, and that would place me right in the hands of the other men. So, my alternative was to creep up on Cobo, catch him by surprise, and try to get his gun away from him. But, where was it? Noticing the small bulge at his waist under his coat I determined that had to be it.

Scooting by inches on my back to the edge of the tarp, I kept my eye on him. He was so close that if I sat up, I could almost reach out and touch his leg. My next move would have to be fast and fluid. As hurt as I was, I wasn't sure I could do fluid. Too bad. It was time.

Rolling to my side and on to my knees, I wobbled to a standing position, lunged for Cobo's back, pulled up on his coat with one hand, and grabbed for his gun with the other.

He twisted around before I could get a tight grip on the gun, and it dropped to the ground, sliding past me. Turning, I dove for it, but he was on me before I could reach it. Grabbing me by the back of my shirt, he shoved me to the side and reached down for the gun, just as a loud explosion ripped through the building and Cobo's arm.

Ignoring his gunshot wound, Cobo bent again for his gun, as another shot rang out. The impact of the bullet to his shoulder pitched his body forward. But, again he started for the gun.

"The next one is going to be through your head. Now, back away." It was Malachi.

Looking over at him, Cobo stayed in his bent position.

Did he want to die?

"Back away." Malachi walked toward him, his gun trained on him.

Concentrating his empty black eyes on Malachi, Cobo waited a few beats, then straightened up and pressed his hand into the bullet wounds on his arm. No. I guess not.

Malachi kicked the gun to a waiting uniformed officer. He was one of several, plus a few men in street clothes, who had poured into the building.

"Tell the paramedics to get in here," Malachi said to them as they hurried over to us. Dragging a chair over to Cobo and pressing him down into it, he nodded at a young female officer, and said, "Watch him, Silva."

Trembling so much I could barely control my limbs, I had pushed myself into a sitting position, but was too weak to stand. Malachi walked over and knelt down beside me. "You okay?"

"Not so much."

"Bring blankets." He glanced up at the officer standing closest to us. "That looks like a pretty good whack." He leaned around to inspect the wound on the back of my head.

"It's throbbing a lot," I said between chattering teeth, closing my eyes, and reaching back to touch my matted hair for the first time. Keeping my eyes closed and breathing deep, it took all my strength to quell the roiling in my stomach. "Carrick kicked me in the chest." I gingerly touched my fingers to it. "And I sliced my ankle."

"You *are* a mess." Malachi set his palm on my forearm.

Opening my eyes, I saw he was smiling softly at me. That did it. I took in a ragged breath, the dam broke, and the tears poured forth from my eyes. I was indeed a mess.

Feeling Malachi wrap a thick blanket over my shoulders, I put my hands to my face, trying to control my sobs.

When I finally quieted, Malachi said, "I know this is hard right now, but we need to move on this, and I have to ask you some questions. Do you think you're up to answering them?"

I nodded. "Can I get some water?"

"Sure, let's get you to a chair. Can you walk?"

"I think so, but I may need some help."

Grabbing my elbow, Malachi steadied me as I stood up, and held on to me until I reached the chair. Handing me a water bottle he had taken from an officer, he pulled another chair over and positioned it opposite mine.

Before he could begin his questioning, two paramedics showed up and began working on Cobo. "Just a minute." He walked over to the men in street clothes who I assumed must be undercover like him. After that, he talked to the officer he had identified as Silva, and sat back down in front of me.

"You said Carrick had kicked you. He was here?"

"Yes."

"How long ago did he leave?"

"I don't know, maybe twenty minutes."

"Did he give any indication about where he was headed?"

"Not really. He told Cobo that after he killed me he needed to get back to the laborers, and someone needed to hunt down Brandon."

"Did you hear anything else while you were locked in the Moran house or here that you think might help us?"

"You knew I was there?"

"Martin Moran told us."

"He went to the police." I sighed. "Was he able to find Brandon?"

"No." He dismissed the question, focused on his immediate concerns. "What else did you hear them say, Sydney?"

"Cobo knew a lot about what I'd been doing, that I'd seen someone in Manhattan about human trafficking, and that I'd been talking to a friend in L.A. about it. That means their gang has people there, right? I'm worried about my friend."

"I'm afraid so. We've got people in L.A. on it, but it'd be best if she left for now. And you best disappear for a while also. This has been a long and involved operation, and we're close, but it's not over."

"My God! I have to call her." I looked around reflexively for my purse. My gut tightened at the memory of Cobo taking it from me. "They have my phone! That means they know all my contacts. They could go after every one of them!"

"We'll do our best to see they don't. But, you're going to have to give us all the information you can remember from your contact list."

With the way my head was throbbing, I didn't see how that was possible.

"Sydney." Malachi moved to the edge of his chair. "There are more paramedics coming. You need to be seen at a hospital. I'm going to assign an officer to you, and guards, if needed. But, as soon as you're able, you need to get out of the area. The officer will help you with the logistics."

"Carrick knew about you too. Did they get that off my phone?"

"No. He'd figured me out a while ago."

"But, why did he let you get away with being around Bridie's? And, if you knew about him, why didn't you do something about it sooner?"

"With him it was probably a matter of keeping your friends close and your enemies closer. For us, it's timing," was his vague answer.

"So, he's *Rock*, right?"

"Yep. Carrick."

"Huh?"

"It means *rock* in Gaelic."

"Clever."

"Yeah, he's a real Einstein." He stood up. "I gotta go. If you think of anything else, tell the officer, and go over your contact list with him as soon as possible."

"Okay. Will I see you again?"

"You should hope not."

I didn't know about that. I felt a lot better thinking he was somewhere lurking in the shadows watching out for me. I pulled the blanket tighter. "Find Brandon, okay? He's not all bad."

"Oh, we'll find him." He stepped away and walked toward the waiting plainclothes officers.

Did that mean Malachi was going to help him, or lock him up?

CHAPTER FIFTEEN

When they finally released me from the hospital it was already midmorning Sunday. Mr. Bumbles and Alice had been stranded in the apartment since Friday night. At best, I would find it a mess from a dearth of pee breaks. At worst, I would find my animals collapsed from neglect. Accompanied by my assigned plainclothes officer Alex Patello, I cracked the door, and as always, the pessimist, I expected the worst.

"Mr. Bumbles," I called out.

No response.

Rushing in, I swept the room. Alice, curled up on the corner of the couch, rolled to her back expecting a tummy rub when I stroked her head. "You haven't suffered much." I looked over at her full water and food bowls. "But, where's your buddy?" I noticed Mr. B's bowls were missing.

"My cousin must have my dog." I sighed in relief. "After I get changed, would you mind if I go up there by myself to explain things? It might make it easier."

"I'll need to walk you to the door first, check it out, but then I can wait back here."

"Thanks. I'll be out in a few minutes."

Oh my God! I sucked in my breath at the frightening image reflected back at me from the mirror. I didn't know how Patello could look at me with a straight face. They had cleaned up the wound on the back of my head, but my hair was still matted in some spots, while poufed out in others. My right eye was swollen from Cobo's slap, and the red ring around my mouth from the tape was still visible.

Turning my ankle to look at their bandaging job, I wondered if it would be all right to get it wet. It had better be, because I was going to anyway.

Wishing I could have taken a whole lot more time under the steaming hot water, but satisfied that with the makeup I applied I looked a whole lot better than when I went in, I hurried out to Patello, anxious to get to Ralph's.

Listening to the jingle of dog tags approaching Ralph's door in response to my knock, I smiled. Mr. B was one of the only lights in my life right then, and I was anxious to see him.

"No, shoo!" we heard a female voice command as the door opened a crack. It was Aunt Felicia. I could tell by the top of her periwinkle wig. "Shoo!"

"Aunt Felicia, it's me, Sydney. Let me help you with Mr. B." I pushed the door open farther and reached down for his collar.

"That dog drools everywhere. It's awful!" She took a tissue out of her sweater pocket, and then scoured her shin and the toe of her spike-heeled shoes with it.

"Sorry. I'll get him out of here. Do you know if he's been walked recently?"

"I have no idea. I'm waiting for Ralph. He said he'd meet me here an hour ago." She looked down at her thin gold watch. "Who's your friend?" She looked up her thin nose at Officer Patello, who was standing behind me.

"This is Alex." I used his first name. I was warned to limit what I said about my situation to only those people who might be in immediate danger, and even with them to be vague about the threat.

"Ma'am." He nodded his head at her.

She pursed her lips and frowned. I swear Aunt Felicia thought she was still forty, maybe even twenty. "There you are." She looked past me.

Turning my head, I saw Ralph approach his front steps. Looking far more disturbed when his eyes landed on his mother than on us, he hesitated before reaching for the rail—weighing the possibility of turning and running, if I knew Ralph.

"You're late," Aunt Felicia narrowed her eyes at him, probably having read his mind.

"Hey, Syd." Ralph ascended the steps, ignoring his mother's jab. "Where you been?" He didn't seem too worried that I had been missing since Friday night.

"Thanks for taking care of Mr. B." I wanted to save my explanations for when I could get him alone.

"He was baying something awful Saturday morning, so I figured I best keep him. Fed Alice too."

"Yeah. I saw that. Thanks."

Acknowledging Patello with a nod, Ralph looked over at me for an introduction.

"This is Alex. Alex, this is Ralph."

"Ralph," Patello said.

"Good to meet you." Ralph walked by me and started to walk by his mother into the house, obviously satisfied I had been with Patello. He needed no more explanation than that.

"Wait, Ralph," I said, "I need to talk with you for a few minutes."

"Well, so do I," Aunt Felicia cut in.

"I'm sorry, Aunt Felicia, this can't wait. But, I promise, I won't keep him long." Turning to Ralph, I asked, glancing down at Mr. B, "When was his last walk?"

"I took him out a couple hours ago."

"Then he's good for a while. Do you have his leash and bowls?"

"Sure. I'll grab 'em." He disappeared inside, with Felicia glaring at his back then at me.

"Really, we won't be long," I reiterated when Ralph returned carrying Mr. B's paraphernalia. "You mind coming to the basement?" I asked him.

"Fine by me." He shrugged.

It wasn't going to be a private discussion after all, as I wasn't going to ask Patello to hang out with Aunt Felicia. I reckoned Ralph should get used to the idea of having an officer around for a while anyway. They told me one would be keeping an eye on the house, whether I was there or not, until Carrick was caught.

"Have a seat, Ralph." I motioned to the couch, and took the opposite end of it, while Patello sat on one of the kitchen chairs a few feet away from us.

"Some very serious things have been going on in the neighborhood." I leaned forward. "And unfortunately, I got involved in them."

"Okay?" Ralph stretched his arm down the back of the couch.

"Remember when I asked you about that teenager named Brandon? We ran into his dad on the way home from the pub one night?"

"Yeah. I guess."

"Well, he was definitely dealing drugs, and was also involved in far more serious crimes." Folding my hands and resting them on my knees, I continued, "I'm not going to tell you all the details. I can't. But the felons he hung with nabbed me and roughed me up. The cops tracked them down and found me, or I'd be dead."

"No kiddin'?"

"No kidding. And, the worst of them are not in custody yet, so to protect myself I have to get out of New York."

"Wow!" Ralph dropped his arm and sat up. "That's crazy!"

"Alex, by the way," I looked over at him, "is an officer assigned to guard me."

Following my glance, Ralph stared at him while it sank in. "Crazy!"

"Unfortunately, Ralph, and I'm so sorry about this, Brandon's buddies know where I live, which puts you at some risk. But, there'll be an officer checking on the house until they're all captured. I've been told they have a lot more to worry about than me, but you still need to be cautious, you know, really be aware of what's going on around you. Got that?"

"Sure."

Digging into his pocket, Patello pulled out a business card and handed it to Ralph. "Here's a number for you to call if you do see anything that doesn't look right, or if you think you're being followed."

"Okay." Ralph leaned back and slid it down the front pocket of his jeans. "But, I'm feeling like I'm in the dark here. You sure there's not more I should know?"

"No." Patello crossed his arms. "The investigation has been jeopardized enough as it is."

Was that a dig at me?

"You go about your normal routine. It's best for everyone," Patello said.

"But, how will I know when it's over. I mean, who's gonna tell me?"

"You'll be told."

"And, I'll call and check in with a burner phone," I said. "The thugs took my cellphone when they captured me, and could possibly have stolen my contact info, but the agents shut down my account, so at least my friends and family won't unknowingly dial felons. Now it's a matter of trying to protect anyone the bad guys might use to get to me. Fortunately, law enforcement is on it."

"So, what now?" Ralph asked.

"So, I get out of Dodge, today. That is, if you can help me. I need the motorhome."

"The motorhome?" Ralph looked the most incredulous he had the entire conversation.

"I'm afraid so. It's the plan I was willing to accept, the only one that includes Mr. B and Alice." I looked over at Patello who scratched his eyebrow. It had been a bit of a struggle getting them to agree, but they couldn't argue with the fact that the likelihood of finding a drug cartel in a KOA campground was pretty slim. "I need you to go to the storage yard, check the tires, oil, and all that. It's working okay, right?"

"Sure, last time I checked."

"We'll follow up behind you as soon as I can pack my things. Grandad's rocker is still in it, right?" Ralph had agreed to borrow a truck and bring the rocker to the basement when I first arrived in New York, and it still hadn't happened. I had no intention of leaving it behind anymore than my animals.

"Yeah." Ralph stood up and headed toward the door. Stopping to look back at me, his eyes as hound dog hurt as Mr. B's, he said, "I never made it to Fort Ticonderoga."

"I know, Ralph. I'm sorry. And, I owe you for rent now, too. I'll make good on it, and somehow get the motorhome back to you." I walked over and patted his back. I would've hugged him, but so far as I could tell, Ralph and his family didn't do hugs. *No kidding.*

I thought of Aunt Felicia waiting upstairs, as I looked through my transom windows to see Ralph's shoes saunter down the street, and away from his mother.

CHAPTER SIXTEEN

"We're back," I said to Alice, who was curled up on the passenger seat, and Mr. B, who was flaked out behind me. "Déjà vu, kids? Yeah, I can't believe it either." Watching yet another car zoom by me in the fast lane as we lumbered along, I couldn't believe it was real. But, it was, and I did it to myself. No denying it. My inability to refrain from sticking my nose in where it doesn't belong got me in trouble once again. So, bye-bye New York, and now what?

The agents that came to the hospital insisted that if I was going to use the motorhome in my disappearing act I had to have an ultimate destination. No problem there. It wasn't like I planned to spend the rest of my life bunking down at national parks and rest stops. It couldn't be L.A., and the thought of holing up in a city where I had no connections, even for a few weeks, left me feeling empty. I was wounded both inside and out, and needed a friendly face. V.A.'s popped to mind, and Noah's, I admit it, and so it didn't take a lot of convincing for me to settle on Harmony.

I told one of the agents I was concerned that some of the people on my contact list were from Harmony, and that

Carrick and his buddies might target them. The agent was fairly confident that a place with more cattle than people was not the best location to set up shop for drug or labor trafficking, and it was a long way to go to chase me down.

Harmony it was, then. Wow!

By the time the agents checked up on me at the hospital, they had already erased the old Sydney Roberts from all things connected to my wallet and phone. They gave me some cash and the three burner phones I had to sign for, and they also put together a temporary driver's license for me–and on a Sunday. And all that time I spent in line at the DMV, who knew it only took being kidnapped by criminals to qualify for the express lane.

The price for all that *help* from the agents? Inclusion on the witness list when the gang members faced the judge and jury. It was not something I was looking forward to, yet I was enough of a justice freak that I would relish watching Cobo and Carrick squirm.

I wondered also if despite their take on Harmony the agents considered me bait. It wasn't out of the question that Carrick would go to great lengths to see he never had to face a jury, and I was one of the few "civilians" who could identify him as the head of the cartel.

With the Interstate sliding underneath me for mile after endless mile there was plenty of time to crank up the volume on the burner phone, set it on my lap, and run through the list of people who were owed an explanation for my disappearance and reappearance, vague though I was told it should be.

My boss Collette was far more understanding than I expected, but then, she should have been. I was good at my job. I also needed that job, and was relieved when she agreed to allow me to skip the trips into the office, and let me finish my latest assignment strictly as a telecommuter. She was also open to the same arrangement on subsequent assignments, until my "family emergency" was resolved. I led her to believe it shouldn't be too long before I was back in New York, but truthfully, with the Atlantic at my back and my nose pointed west, I had no idea when or if I would return.

My next call was to Vincent, and I was glad when he picked up his extension. Carrick's gang knew about my visit to the anti-trafficking office, and I was worried it might be one of their first targets.

"Vincent here," he answered.

"Vincent, hi, it's Sydney Roberts, we met at your office."

"Sure, I know. We talked about your doing some editing and writing on the newsletter."

"Yeah. That's right." Of course he would remember that. "And, I still plan on following through on my commitment, but it may be awhile. I'm headed out of town because I'm on the radar of a trafficking gang, and I'm afraid your office is too. I'm pretty sure they followed me there. I'm sorry I put you all in danger."

"Wouldn't be the first time." He didn't sound very worried. "Our work has us on a lot of radar screens, and not just in this country."

"But, what do you do about it? I mean, how do you protect yourselves?"

"We work with law enforcement, and we ask for their presence when needed."

"They may be more present for the next few weeks, until the gang I collided with is broken up and behind bars."

"You mean you had an actual run-in with them?"

"You could say that." I rubbed my fingers across the sore knot at the back of my head.

"Sounds like a great story for the newsletter."

"Really? That's what you think of first?" I smiled into the phone.

"Sure." I could tell he was smiling too.

"I'll wait until I hear there's a happy ending before I write it. How about that?"

"Agreed."

"And, in the meantime, keep an eye out, okay, Vincent?"

"Sure. You too. And, stay in touch."

"Will do." I was determined I would. I may have been running away from trouble then, but I wasn't abandoning the battle. I was long overdue for joining the good guys in the good fight.

Dori had always been part of the good fight. I could picture her standing up to her polygamous parents to defend Luke from the time she was very young. In fact, when I called her from the hospital to warn her someone in the women's shelter where she volunteered may have connections to the traffickers, she refused to leave town. I didn't have time to argue with her then, but had plenty on my ride, and I wasn't going to hear of her staying there.

It took me almost the entire width of Indiana to convince her the gang was a real threat to her and her brother, but she finally gave in–for Luke's sake. She even agreed to return to Harmony to outwait the threat there with me. It would be an opportunity for her to check on Ruthie and some of the other victims of polygamy she had been working with.

I told her I was coming to pick her and Luke up, and would be there in three or four days. I was taking no chance she would change her mind and stay in Southern California.

My problem was that in order to get there, I would need a car. My Moby Dick RV was too slow, too big, and too ugly. By the time I reached Harmony, I'd want to abandon the thing for something that could get me to L.A.–fast. And, for that I was going to have to talk to Cal.

Cal, jeez, how was it that I was once again going to have to ask prison-jumpsuit Cal for a favor? But, where would I have been without those favors? He had chased away the evil-intentioned Bailey brats, fixed the motorhome, and let me park it in his yard. He had been good to me. I needed to keep that in mind.

After a short stop to resupply the Fritos and gas, I made my call to Cal. Drumming my fingers along the top of the steering wheel, I waited several rings for him to pick up. I was just about to give up when he answered, "Yeah?"

"Cal, this is Sydney Roberts, you know, with the motorhome you fixed."

"Ain't heard from you in a piece. Where you been?"

"I moved to New York, remember. That's where I went when I left Harmony."

"Thought you said you was goin' to Boston."

"No. It was New York. I've been in New York."

He clicked his tongue against the top of his mouth. "I'm pretty darn sure you said Boston."

"No Cal, it was New York!" I snapped.

"Still techy, it seems."

"I'm not techy, er touchy," I ratcheted down my volume. "It's just I wasn't in Boston."

"Fine by me."

"Anyway," I shook my head, trying to focus on the reason for my call, "I'm on my way back to Harmony in the motorhome, and ..."

"How's she runnin'?" he interrupted.

"Fine. Just fine," I said and added, after an expectant silence from his end, "You did a great job on the repair."

"She was a tough case, that one."

"I know. You really spent a lot of time on it." Oh my God! I was going to be in Utah by the time he let me get to my point.

"Yeah, a real tough one."

"So Cal, I'm calling because when I get to Harmony I'm going to need a place to park the motorhome and wondered if you'd mind my keeping it in your yard again?"

"Got your hound with you?"

"Yeah, and the cat too."

"Good. That's good."

"I'm glad you think so." I wondered what my animals had to do with anything. "So, would it be all right?"

"I don't see why not."

"But here's the other thing. I need to leave for Los Angeles right after I get to Harmony, and I don't want to use the motorhome. Do you have a car at your place I could rent? It would only be for as long as it takes for me to get there and back."

"Hmm." He hesitated, clicking his tongue again. "Yeah, I got a machine just needs a bit of cobbling."

"Okay? Is it reliable?"

"Course," he said in an indignant tone.

"Great!" I quickly covered my doubt. He really had done a good job on the motorhome. Patting the dashboard, I thought I needed to keep the faith. "I should be there day after tomorrow at the latest."

Day after tomorrow. Back in Harmony. Back in Noah land. We hadn't talked at all since I left. I believed that a clean break was the best way to go. With him attached to Harmony, it would be impossible for a relationship to develop, and I hadn't expected to see him again—ever. But, it was funny how when it came time to decide where to land, it was on his runway.

CHAPTER SEVENTEEN

After maneuvering the motorhome into "our spot" in Cal's yard and doing a bit of tidying up, I stepped out of it into the fading sunlight. Cal's coonhounds surrounded me, eagerly anticipating the return of Mr. Bumbles. Mr. B was pretty eager himself, his tail thumping as he took in his doggy paradise before being enveloped by his pack.

Doggy paradise, indeed. Scanning the yard, I wondered how many decades Cal had been accumulating his rust piles. He certainly hadn't made any dents in them in the weeks I had been gone. Even though the fresh paint on the motorhome had erased all traces of the Bailey boys' tagging job, it still fit perfectly into the junkyard tableau.

Heading for the shop to look for Cal, I found him, or at least his bottom half, sticking out from under a compact silver hatchback with missing hubcaps. "Cal," I said softly, recalling the time I startled him when he was working on a truck and he hit his head.

"Huh?" came a muffled response.

"Is this the car?"

"What'd ya say?" He rolled out from under it, stopping right by my legs and staring straight up at me, his face streaked with grease.

"Is this the car? The one you're going to rent to me?"

"Yup."

"Is something wrong with it?" I was hopeful it hadn't needed more than the little "cobbling" he talked about.

"No." He narrowed his eyes at me. "Why'd ya ask that?"

"Because you're working on it." Wasn't it obvious?

"I saw to her. She's right as rain. Just checking the linkage."

"Oh, good. It's okay to take to L.A., then?"

"You can drive her clear to Argentinia and back, and she'll give you no trouble. These things were designed to go half a million miles. Gets good gas mileage too."

"L.A.'s far enough." I had no interest in compressing myself into the tiny car all the way to Argentin*ia*. "I really appreciate your doing this for me, and letting me park the motorhome here again. When I get back, I'll look around for another place to park it."

"Stay long as you want. No skin off my nose."

"Thanks for that. I do have one other favor." I looked down at the deep creases radiating from Cal's gray eyes. "I need to leave Mr. Bumbles behind, Alice too. Will you watch them for me? It should only be for a day."

"Sure." He wiped his forehead with the back of his arm.

"That's great. Thank you." The last thing I needed was to bring a slobbery dog and angry cat along. As much as Luke liked my animals, it wouldn't be a fun ride back to Harmony with him and them stuffed into the tiny back seat. "I'll let you get back to your work. I'm going to Dusty's to grab something to eat. But, the car will be ready in the morning?"

"She'll be ready in a few, but I wouldn't be taking off just now. Least not with *your* sense of direction. It's gonna be dark soon."

"What?" I frowned at his knock at my navigational skills.

He winked and slid back under the car.

Cal had a sense of humor. How about that?

I could smell simmering marinara almost before I saw Dusty's–yum–buffalo Bolognese. I hadn't thought about the dish while I was in New York, but now that it was within reach, I was salivating.

I was happy to see the familiar long bony back of Patrick Crane seated at the counter when I walked in. I was hoping he would be there. I wanted to give him a heads up about my run-in with the traffickers. Even though the agents thought there was little chance of the creeps showing up in Harmony, Patrick needed to know they could trace me there.

"You're back." Patrick looked surprised when I slid onto the stool next to his.

"I am."

"Didn't expect to see you again."

"Didn't expect to be here."

A waitress with gray roots and a no-nonsense attitude set a glass of water and a menu in front of me.

"No need." I handed the menu back to her. "I know what I want."

"Shoot," she said, her pad and pen poised.

"Buffalo Bolognese with a salad, balsamic dressing on the side. Thanks."

"Anything to drink?"

"Water's fine."

"Right-O." She flipped around and handed the order through the pass-through. I assumed the muscular forearm that grabbed it was Dusty's, who I planned on talking to after I ate. I wanted to let him know that Dori and Luke were coming back for a while. I was responsible for her having to leave L.A. and her job there, and as paternal as he felt about them, I was hoping he would give them some temporary work.

"What brings you back here?" Patrick asked then took a sip of his coffee.

"I need to talk to you about that." Checking to make sure the waitress wasn't in earshot, I twisted to face him, and said softly, "While I was in New York I stumbled into the midst of a human trafficking cartel. They discovered I was aware of their activity, and my purse and phone ended up in their hands. The police told me that for my safety I needed to leave town for a while."

"Dangerous stuff," he said with more than mild curiosity in his eyes. "And, they were satisfied with just your phone and purse?"

"Not exactly."

"I didn't think so."

"I'm heading to L.A. early tomorrow morning to pick up Dori and Luke and bring them back here, because I unfortunately asked Dori to talk to the people in the women's shelter where she volunteers about the traffickers. They somehow got wind of it, which puts her at risk. When I get back I'll fill you in on the whole story, in private," I added when I saw the waitress walk our way with my salad.

Patrick let out a low whistle.

"I know, it's bad," I said when we were alone again. "One of the things I'm most worried about is that the traffickers may be aware of my Harmony connection. I wanted you to know that in the event anyone pops up here that doesn't look like your normal tourist."

"Like we get tourists." He smiled.

"True." I smiled back. "It's not exactly a vacation destination."

"I'll be on the lookout, though."

"Thanks, and I'll call you from the road if there are any new developments." I reached into my purse, pulled out my phone, and showed it to him. "It's a burner phone. Makes me feel a little like a criminal myself."

"You never know about you redheads."

"I suppose not," I said, thinking that the speed at which he reached the red hair comment may have set a record.

After I ate, I talked to Dusty, and he was more than happy to find some work for Dori and Luke at the diner, if only for a little while. I didn't offer an explanation for their or my return, other than it was an extended visit. He didn't seem to need one.

My last stop for the evening was V.A.'s. Her place was still my only option for a decent shower, and knowing that, I called her from the road that morning. She didn't require much of an explanation either, nor did hearing from me faze her, even though I was supposedly out of her life forever. Must be nice to take life as it comes, rather than my approach, which is to scrutinize it like a chimp scouring its mate's fur for fleas.

"Come sit a spell, Missy," V.A. said when I emerged from her bathroom. Standing in the kitchen, she gestured to the table as I approached. "Hot chocolate?" She walked over to the stove.

"That sounds really good. Yeah, thanks." I sat down.

"I like to treat myself to it when the weather takes a turn to the cool side." She filled two mugs. "Marshmallows?"

"Why not."

"How'd you end up in the ranks of the walking wounded?" she asked, with her back to me.

"What do you mean?" I was dumbfounded she somehow could tell I was still hurting from the abuse I took from Cobo and Carrick.

"How'd you get that cut on your ankle, the bruises on your arms, and the bump on the back of your head?" She set the mug on the table and stood over me, waiting for my answer.

Damn. Why hadn't I put on my socks and sweater before I left the bathroom? And, how could she have possibly seen my scalp through my hair? "You can't see the knot." I looked up, deciding to challenge her.

"No, but I saw you wince when you touched it."

I hadn't been able to keep my hands off the egg at the back of my skull, constantly checking it for size and soreness. "You better take a seat. I'll try not to go into too much detail, but the story's a long one." There was no point in keeping the events of the last few weeks from V.A. I had planned on telling her at least part of it anyway, because her number was one of the ones in my phone when Cobo took it from me.

So much for thinking I was only going to stick to a shortened version of the events. By the time I caught my breath, I had purged every last detail, and felt a whole lot lighter for it. V.A. was one of those people with so much confidence it made you feel like when you were around her everything was going to be all right. And, it was the first time in a long while I dared entertain that belief.

"Well, Missy, you did get yourself into it a bit of a pickle."

"You could say that." I loved her phraseology–and penchant for understatement–and by then had gotten used to the Missy thing.

"So, now what?"

"I'm leaving for L.A. in the morning to pick up Dori and Luke and bring them back here, and then I guess we'll lie low until we get the all clear from law enforcement."

"You all set for a place to stay?"

"I think so. Dori said they could bunk with her old neighbors, and I'm back in the motorhome. I was thinking of asking around about moving it to another spot, but Mr. Bumbles is so happy with Cal's coonhounds, I almost hate to do that to him."

"It's an entertaining place for a dog, that's for sure. I'd let you park out back of this place, but there's not much there but red dust and sage."

"That's all right. So long as you don't mind my using your shower every once in a while, I'll probably leave the motorhome where it is."

"You could park her at Noah's, you know. He has lots of open land, and Trudy would probably enjoy the company."

Feeling my face grow hot the second I heard Noah's name, I concentrated on keeping my voice steady. "No, really, we're good with Cal's."

"Haven't talked to him, huh?"

"No." Oh boy. That was an unexpected turn in the conversation.

"Curious, considering your partiality for him the last time you were here."

"I wasn't partial to him. I couldn't be when I knew I was never coming back," I said too quickly. My face must have been crimson by then. When had V.A. decided to become a Yenta? That was the last thing I expected out of that practical woman.

"And then *never* came."

She had me on that one. "Well, yes."

Taking a sip from her mug, she let the topic of Noah hang in the air between us, but said no more on it.

Checking the dashboard and controls to familiarize myself with the car Cal rented to me, I yawned and tried to clear the cobwebs from my head. Dawn was just creeping over the red rocks as I turned the key in the ignition and nosed onto Main Street. I left Alice curled up on my bed, in the same spot I was likely to find her on my return. Mr. B was enjoying a sleepover in the shop with his buddies, so he was more than set. It was a relief not to have to worry about them. I needed to focus on reaching L.A. as quickly as possible, and getting Dori and Luke out of there.

Never a beehive of activity, Harmony was dead quiet that time of day. There were some lights on at Dusty's, and I noticed his silhouette moving around in the dining area as I passed by. Long days were the price of being in the restaurant business; something Dusty never seemed to mind. The place was his life.

When I turned to look back at the road, I noticed the headlights of a truck slowly approaching. I was immediately on alert. There was a good chance Carrick's people would search for me despite the agents' reassurance. I gripped the steering wheel, prepared to speed to safety with the horn blaring.

Driving in a zigzag pattern, because I heard somewhere that was the best way to avoid being hit by bullets, I lowered my body in the seat.

When the truck slowed to a crawl as it pulled even with me, I glanced over, started to accelerate, and then stamped on the brake. It was Noah. *Shit.* I was hoping to put off seeing him until long after I returned.

Stopping and turning off his engine, he stepped out of his truck, and walked over to me.

After I rolled down my window, he said, as casually as we had just seen each other the day before, "I thought that was you. Why in the heck were you driving like that?"

"Hard to explain." I straightened up in my seat.

"I'm listening." He reached down to open the door. "Or *will* when you get out."

"But, we're right in the middle of the road."

"You see any traffic?"

"No." I looked up and down Main Street. There wasn't even any tumbleweed moving about.

"I think we're all right."

"Okay." I stepped out of the car, closed the door, and then leaned against it, trying to keep some space between us.

"Hello, by the way." He smiled.

"Hello to you too." I smiled back. I couldn't help myself. I was really glad to see him. Damn.

"You were going to tell me about the unique way you were driving."

"Yes, well you see, when I was in New York, I kind of got mixed up with these human traffickers, and when I saw you coming at me so slowly, I was scared maybe you were them."

"So, you what? Thought that by driving like you were in a bumper car, they might not notice?"

"No. I heard if you zigzag, you're a harder target to hit."

"I think that's for people, not automobiles. Even a lousy shot would have an easy time hitting the broadside of a car."

"Oh."

"Couldn't find work with a publisher, so you joined a criminal organization?" His eyes danced.

"No! That's not what I meant." I shifted my weight to my feet, straightened my back and crossed my arms. "There's a lot more to it than that."

"Which I would know about if you had kept in touch," he lowered his voice and took a step toward me so we were only inches apart. He wasn't wearing his hat, and apparently hadn't had time for a haircut in a while, as strands of his hair curled down his neck to his shirt collar.

Oh boy. My weakness. I dragged my eyes from his neck. "I, uh ... Wait! You didn't stay in touch either."

"Didn't need to." He ran his hands over my shoulders and down my arms.

I dropped my arms to my side. "You didn't *need to*?"

"No." He slid his hands around my back and drew me to him. "You were coming back."

"No. I wasn't."

"Sure you were." He combed the hair around my ear with his fingers. "You changed it."

"Yeah." The warmth radiating from his body felt heavenly against the sharp chill of the autumn air.

"Mmm." He lowered his head, kissed my forehead, the tip of my nose, and my lips.

How could he do this? Just pick up right where we left off? I lapped up his attentions like the runt in a litter of Labrador retrievers. When he finally pulled back, reality set in–hard. I was on a mission, for goodness sake. What was I doing making out in the middle of Main Street at dawn when I needed to get to L.A.? "Wait," I stepped out of his hold. "I need to go. I'm on my way to pick up Dori and Luke, and want to try to do it all in one day, if I can."

"Because?"

"The traffickers may be after Dori." I put my hand on the door handle. "Ask V.A. about it. She'll fill you in."

"I'd rather hear it from you."

"Then, you're going to have to wait a day."

"Any more than that, and I'm sending the cavalry out after you."

"That won't be necessary."

"With you, I'm never sure."

"I'll be fine, really." I was offended at his lack of faith.

"All right then. I'll expect you for dinner tomorrow night. "You'll be providing the entertainment."

"I will?" I blushed, my mind going straight to the bedroom.

"Yes. Your story, I'm looking forward to hearing it." He raised his eyebrows.

"Right, my story." I knew full well he could read my mind.

As I opened the door and folded myself into the driver's seat, he leaned down and rested his palms on the doorframe. "No motorhome?"

"Too slow. I borrowed this from Cal."

"And, you aren't going to make any unscheduled stops in the desert, right?"

"No. Jeez. You get lost once, and no one ever lets you forget it. I know where I'm going." Fastening my seatbelt, I looked up at Noah after he closed the door. "Why are you out so early, anyway?"

"I heard Dusty was going to be serving something special for breakfast and there might be a crowd." He winked, tapped the door twice, turned and walked back to his truck.

Wait. Had V.A. told him I was in Harmony? I put the car in gear and drove off wondering ...

CHAPTER EIGHTEEN

In my conversation with Dori on my way to L.A., she confessed she was making one last trip to the women's shelter, after I told her to stay away. She insisted on talking to one of the women she had connected with to reassure her she would be back soon.

I thought that *soon* might have been a little optimistic. I hadn't been in contact with Malachi at all–I hadn't expected to be–corralling a worldwide trafficking ring was a Herculean task that he warned me was going to take time.

Dori told me to meet her at her apartment. She and Luke were packed up and would be ready to go when I arrived. Fortunately, most of their things were still in Harmony, stored in her neighbor's garage. She planned to make L.A. her home, but had decided to stick with a monthly lease until she got the lay of the land. Thank God. Looking over my shoulder into the miniscule back seat of the car, I knew there was no way I was going to fit more than the three of us and a little luggage into it.

Rapping on Dori's door for the second time, I began to worry I had the wrong address. Double-checking my note, I knocked again. As I stood staring at the faded gray door, I caught a whiff of what I guessed was kimchi. The cultural and ethnic tides that ebbed and flowed through L.A.'s neighborhoods always fascinated me. One group would dominate a district for a decade or two, and then drift up a hillside, as another surged in from distant and often hostile lands to take its place. The amalgam of stragglers in the flatland districts who chose not to join the exodus up the hill created a fusion of sights and smells. It made for great people-watching from modest sidewalk eateries.

When there was still no answer at the door, I called Dori on her cellphone. She was just leaving the shelter, and said she'd be there in twenty to thirty minutes, depending on the bus. She also said Luke was home, but may be hesitant to answer the door. After saying good-bye to her, I knocked again, and called out, "Luke, it's me, Sydney. We met in Harmony. You told me about Alaska, remember?"

The door opened a crack and Luke peeked out.

"Hi, Luke. I'm here to pick you and Dori up and take you to Harmony."

"Dori's not here," he said not opening the door any farther.

"I know. I just talked to her. She'll be home in a few minutes. May I come in?"

Stepping back into the apartment, he left me to open the door.

As I entered, he walked over to one of the two front windows. Sitting down in a kitchen chair that had been moved under it, he pulled the vertical blinds apart two inches and stared out.

Okay? What's this about? "Are you watching for Dori?"

"No." He didn't look away from the window.

"Then, what are you doing?"

"Looking for the men."

"The men?" Goose bumps prickled my hairline. "What men?"

"The men in the car."

"Luke." I walked over to stand in front of him, but not too close. "Would you let go of the blinds for a minute, please, and tell me what you mean. *What men?*"

Dropping his hands to his lap, he turned in my direction, but didn't look up at me. "The men in the black SUV."

"Are they there now?" My heart stopped. That couldn't be good.

"No. They left."

"How long ago?"

"At 11:52 a.m."

"Wow. That's precise, Luke. You'd make a great detective." I tried to keep my tone light, so he wouldn't notice my rising panic. "How long were they there?"

"I don't know. I didn't notice them until 9:17 a.m."

"What do you think they were doing?"

"Staking out the joint."

If I hadn't been so worried, I would have smiled at that response. Clearly, Luke had seen a few gangster movies. "You mean, this joint?"

"Yes."

Oh my God! "How do you know that?"

"They kept looking this way."

"Have you seen them before?"

"No."

Controlling my rising panic, I gestured to the bulging duffle bags that were sitting by the door. "Let's carry these things down to my car so we're ready to leave when Dori gets here. And we need to move fast, okay, Luke? Those men may be trouble for us."

"Okay, yeah." He hurried over to the bags. "But, this one has my Xbox in it. We have to be very careful with it." His concern for his video games apparently trumped his fear of bad guys.

"That's fine. You can put it on the seat next to you, but we gotta go!"

Just as we finished loading the car, we saw Dori step off her bus and hurry toward us.

"Hey, Dori," I said when she reached us, then gave her a quick hug.

"Hey to you too. How was the ride?" She pulled out of my embrace.

Feeling exposed out on the street and pressure to get out of there fast, I ignored her question. "Luke told me that some men have been watching the apartment."

"They were staking out the joint," Luke spoke up.

"What!"

"Yeah. We need to go."

"You got everything out of the apartment?" She looked from one to the other of us.

We nodded our heads.

"I'll just drop the key off at the manager's apartment and we're out of here.

"How 'bout we leave right now and you mail that key back?" I scurried around to the driver's side.

"Right!" Dori widened her dark eyes at me over the top of the car, her sense of urgency catching up to mine.

A sense of relief washed over me as we made our way past the regimental row of apartment buildings on our way to the boulevard that led to the freeway. The faster we put L.A. behind us the better.

That relief was short-lived when I noticed a large black SUV coming up behind us. There had to be thousands of them in L.A., but I wasn't taking any chances. "Dori, Luke, duck down, quick!"

"Duck down?" Luke remained upright.

"Put your head down, Luke!" Dori reached back and patted his leg. She wasn't questioning my command. Thank goodness!

Pulling into one of the driveways wasn't an option. And, there was no way the sorry little putt-putt I was driving could outrun them. Since I had no previous connection to the hatchback, I decided my best chance to escape unnoticed was to drive ten miles above the speed limit, like every other driver on L.A.'s roads when afforded the rare opportunity to have no other vehicle in front of them.

As the gap closed between us, I could see in my rearview mirror that there were two men in the front seat, with all the thug-like qualities to scare the shit out of me. Holding steady to my speed, I forced myself to concentrate on the road. They, on the other hand, pulled within inches of my rear bumper.

That was it. Time to conclude that these were not your average bros, out for a leisurely drive. We were in serious trouble.

Thinking, the hell with you, Noah, I slid down in my seat, pressed down hard on the gas pedal, and began rotating the steering wheel from side to side.

Hearing a pop, I glanced in my rearview mirror to see the passenger thug's hand sticking out the window and pointing a gun at our car. "Shit. Shit. Shit!" When Dori started to raise her head. I shouted, "No! Keep it down! Yours too, Luke!" Sticking with my bumper-car maneuver, and forcing the car up to the fastest speed I could handle, I swerved onto a cross street.

Our luck with the no traffic thing ran out. In front of me, a line of cars stacked behind the red stoplight. My choice was to let them gun us down from behind, swerve around the cars in front of me, or take the sidewalk. I chose the latter, and had just started up the curb when I saw another large black SUV speed toward us, then heard the sickening sound of crashing metal behind us.

I hoped to God the bad guys had run their car into oblivion! I continued my trajectory up the curb, and straight over a large bush. And we would have made the sidewalk too, if not for the decorative boulder in my path, and the car's five-inch clearance.

Slamming my hand on the steering wheel, I shouted, "We gotta get outta here, now! Your side, Dori! Luke, climb out behind her, and stay low! Use the parked cars as a shield!"

Following them out the door, we crouched low and scurried alongside the parked cars. "Keep moving!" I shouted at their backs. "Get to the boulevard! They won't shoot at us there!" Right. Where I got that, I didn't know. I just figured they might be reluctant to shoot off a gun in a crowd. Like they had moral lines they didn't cross! Sure.

Hearing the pop of gunfire behind us, Dori jumped in front of the nearest parked car, dragged Luke with her, and threw her arm over the top of him. I followed them, crouched down, and also threw an arm over Luke. Trying to hear what was going on over the sound of my own hard breathing, I peeked around the hood of the car to see a pair of jean-clad legs rushing toward me. Oh my God. "Move! Move!" I pushed at Luke and Dori. Around the car!" It was too late. The legs were beside me. I wrapped both arms over Luke and held my breath.

A hand gripped onto my shoulder. "Sydney," I heard through the rush of my pulse in my ears.

As the hand tugged on my sweater to get me to stand up, I fought back. There was no way I was going to witness my own execution. They could just shoot me in the back, the cowards.

"Sydney." I heard, louder this time.

Wait. What? I opened my eyes and peeked over my shoulder. "Malachi?" I let Luke go, and turned in his direction.

Offering his hand, he said, "It's safe to get up now."

"You sure?"

"I'm sure."

Putting my hand in his, I let him pull me up, then I turned and offered my hand to Luke. He ignored it and stood up on his own, looking back over the roof of the car. "They nabbed them," he said.

As Dori stood up, she said, "They sure did."

Following their glance, I took in the *Five O'clock News* footage that was unfolding on the street. The SUV that was tailing me had come to a halt angled into the oncoming traffic, having been hit from behind by yet another black SUV, occupied by undercover cops. The SUV that had been coming toward me was nose into the thugs' vehicle, whose occupants were slowly stepping down, arms in the air. A half-dozen plainclothes officers in bulletproof vests had guns trained on them, and grabbed them by the arms and handcuffed them as soon as they cleared their car. There were several uniformed cops at the periphery of the scene, holding back the crowd that had started to form.

"You're here." I turned my eyes on Malachi.

"Yeah, and I thought you were supposed to be in Utah."

"I needed to pick them up. The traffickers know about my connection to them."

"Ya think?" He scowled at me, and looked over at the men being hauled away.

"They were in danger." I felt my cheeks get hot at his indictment of my stating the obvious.

"We had it covered."

"How was I supposed to know that? I haven't heard from any of you in days." Now he was just making me mad.

"I'm Dori," she interrupted, frowning at me, then stepping by me and holding her hand out to Malachi. "And this is my brother Luke." She nodded back at him as Malachi shook her hand.

"A pleasure," Malachi said, acknowledging Luke with a nod.

"Thank you for coming to our rescue. We would've been in major trouble if you hadn't shown up when you did." She looked over at me expectantly.

"Yes. Thank you." I felt like my mother was reprimanding me.

"You're most welcome." Malachi allowed a trace of his Irish accent to come through, and an Irish gleam to cross his eyes as he looked from me to Dori. He held on to her hand a couple more beats, then let it go. "You're driving straight to Utah?"

"Do we still need to?" Dori asked. "Now that you've caught them." She watched a cop put one of the gang members into the back of his cruiser.

"It's not over." He looked the same direction.

"Carrick?" I asked.

"Not yet." He looked over at me.

"Damn."

"Will you let us know as soon as it's okay for us to come back to L.A.? I don't want to stay away any longer than I have to," Dori said.

"You like this place, huh?" Malachi looked over at the crowd.

"Sure. Don't you?"

"Too much sunshine." He smiled.

"Oh, so you're one of those moody types who prefers to live under a blanket of dark skies and damp air."

"I'm Irish."

"One winter of walking through warm sand in bare feet, and I bet you'd be a convert."

"I don't know. I'm pretty set in my ways."

Okay? You two are flirting? Now? Weren't villains just shooting at us? I caught Dori's eye. She pretended not to notice. Turning to Malachi, I said, "Do you think I did any damage to the car?"

"The taillight's not looking too good. They must have shot it out." He glanced over at the hatchback. "You should probably get it fixed before you get back on the road."

"Can't take the time. I want to make it to Harmony tonight."

"I get it. Just be sure to check your rearview mirror a lot."

"I know how to drive." I crossed my arms.

"Okaaay?" He drew the word out and looked pointedly at the little hatchback balancing on the curb.

"I was being chased." I threw my arms out, palms up. "And, maybe if you and the bad guys weren't all driving the same large black SUVs I would have known it was you in the car coming at me, and not someone wanting to kill us. Really, you need to send out a memo—all good guys drive white; all bad guys drive black. Like in the Westerns with their cowboy hats, so the rest of us can tell you apart."

"I'll take that under advisement." He turned up the corner of his mouth.

"Good." I smiled. "You do that."

"I'll have one of the officers back your car onto the street and make sure it's drivable," he offered.

"Thanks."

"We're going to need statements from all of you about today, but I won't hold you up now. I need to get going, and you should clear out of here."

"Do you think the traffickers know I'm staying in Utah?" I asked.

"Hard to tell. But, they've got a lot bigger problems to deal with than you, so you should be okay."

"I don't like the word *should* as much as *will.*"

"Just keep a lookout."

"I'm a good lookout," Luke spoke up for the first time.

"Good to hear. I'll be expecting a full report of everything that has happened," Malachi took on a serious tone.

"I will do that. Yes. I remember everything," Luke said.

"And, you'll help them watch for trouble."

"Yes."

"Good."

"So, someone will call when it's all over, right?" Dori asked.

"I'll deliver the news myself."

He never made that offer to me.

"Well then, good luck, good luck."

"Do we need it?" Dori asked.

"No. You three will be more than fine. It's just an Irish way to say good-bye."

"Good luck, good luck, then." Dori held up her palm.

"Good luck, good luck," Luke echoed.

Malachi looked from Luke to Dori, with his eyes resting an extra second on her, then hurried off.

CHAPTER NINETEEN

Other than the broken taillight and a teensy dent in the front end from my run-in with the boulder, the hatchback was in pretty good shape. It was going to be well after dark by the time we arrived in Harmony, but not so late that I'd be falling asleep at the wheel.

Both Dori and Luke had taken their turns napping, but were awake again, with Luke heavily involved in a video game. He wasn't missing much. The road between Los Angeles and Southern Utah was a lot like the old quote about flying–hours of interminable boredom punctuated by a few moments of terror–with Las Vegas filling in for the terror part.

"So, Malachi," Dori said, finally bringing him up. I had been wondering how long it would take her. She liked to maintain a detached façade, but I could tell he had piqued her interest.

"Yes?"

"What was your deal with him in New York?"

"He was posing as a singer in the Irish pub where my cousin and his friends hang out. It was his cover. I told you that, right?"

"Yeah. You mentioned it. And?"

"And, he saved me from being shot by Cobo and his men. You know that too."

"I mean personally. What was your relationship with him?"

"There was no personally." I glanced over at her through the waning light.

"Doesn't seem like it. You were too testy with each other."

"So testy equates to there being something between two people?"

"Absolutely. Where there's testy, there's heat."

"Is that a Dori-ism?"

"Sure." She smiled.

"Well, in this case, it's false. All his heat was directed at you today."

"No!"

"Yeah. And you felt it."

She was quiet for a moment. "It wasn't just me thinking that, then?" She dropped the pretense.

"No. There was something there."

"No use putting any emotional energy into that one, though. Between habitats and job descriptions, we're thousands of miles apart."

"So, you're giving up before you start?"

"Pretty much. Besides, I have major plans on the horizon." She tucked one leg under the other and turned to face me.

"Oh yeah, what kind?"

"Cambodia."

"Cambodia? Wow! I wasn't expecting that one."

"It's one of the hot spots for human trafficking. I've been talking to people at the shelter about it."

"How are you going to pull that one off?"

"I've been looking into the non-profit groups working there. I plan to save my money and volunteer with one of them for a few weeks. There's just too much need for me to live my cushy life and not do something about it." She put her palm to her chest.

"Your life isn't cushy!" Being shunned by her polygamist group and having to work as a waitress to support her and Luke was hardly a *cushy* life.

"Sure it is, when you open your eyes to the way billions of other people live. And none of that is going to change unless more of the privileged help."

"You've already helped a lot—Ruthie, the women at the shelter, and you're what? Twenty-four?"

"That's not enough for me. I spent way too much time stuck in a very small corner of the world. No more. I want to get my hands dirty, educate myself, and open people's eyes to what's going on outside their own little worlds."

"What about Luke?"

"Harry's watching him for me while I'm in Cambodia. As far as the rest of it goes, we'll figure it out as we go along."

"My boyfriend Harry? You already talked to him about it?"

"Yeah. And, he's not your boyfriend anymore, remember?"

"True." I drummed my fingers on the steering wheel.

"Luke really likes him."

"He *is* a great guy."

"No doubt," she said and then changed the subject. "Didn't you mention you were going to do some writing for that non-profit in New York that deals with human trafficking?"

"Yeah." I glanced over at her. What was she getting at?

"Cambodia would be a great topic for an article." She cocked her head.

"You're suggesting I go with you?"

"Why not? You're a telecommuter now, aren't you? You can do your job anywhere there's Wi-Fi."

"You're going to have to let me think a bit on that one, Dori. I'd like to see Malachi wrap up our *own* traffickers first."

"That's fine." Dori shifted again in her seat and stared out her passenger window at the last of the day's light. She didn't have to say anymore. She'd figured me out well enough to know she'd started my wheels spinning.

The place where I'd spent my entire *cushy* life hadn't been as small as Dori's, but it may well have been for as narrow a worldview as I held. The last few months proved it. My recent experiences and the people I encountered added a lot of new colors to my life's palate. And, I had no desire to crawl back into my gray hole.

One of the things spinning around in that overworked mind of mine was Noah. Where did he fit into it all? I guess beginning the next night I was going to find out.

"I'm running low on gas, and want to fill up so when I return this thing to Cal it has a full tank." I pulled off the freeway on the outskirts of St. George and into the closest gas station to the exit. "Do either of you need to use the bathroom?"

"I better." Dori reached down and picked her purse up off the floorboard. Looking into the back seat, she asked, "How about you, Luke, do you want to go to the bathroom, or want something to eat?"

"I need chips." His downturned face glowed green from his video game screen. I was surprised the batteries hadn't run out hours before.

"Okay, come with me." She opened the door and pushed her seat forward to make way for him to get out.

As I stood at the pump, I arched my back and inhaled deeply. Even over the gas fumes I could smell the tang of sage and mineral-laced dirt. It was cold, but I liked it. It made me feel sharp and alive. Good thing. I was going on thirteen hours of driving, with a shootout sandwiched in between.

Gazing deep into the starry sky, I was amazed at how bright it was, even with the interference of the light from the fringes of St. George. As I dropped my eyes back down to read the meter on the gas pump, I noticed an old four-door sedan pulled up to the pump on the other side of mine. I sensed that someone was looking at me, but the driver was walking into the mart.

Then I glanced into the backseat of the sedan. There staring out at me was Samuel Vaullie. When he saw he had my full attention, he smiled, a crazy malicious smile.

My first thought was to hop in the car, gather up Dori and Luke, and fly out of there. It was a sensible plan, considering Samuel was a murderer, and his buddy in the mart and the one I noticed sitting in the front seat were probably dangerous fanatics like him. But, I wasn't leaving without the license plate number from their car.

Pulling the nozzle out of the tank then scurrying to the driver's seat, I hopped in and started the engine. I could see Dori and Luke's heads through the glass door. Putting the car in gear, I circled around the island of gas pumps, and slowed when I rounded the back of Samuels's car, long enough to read the license plate. Then I started repeating it over and over while I pulled up in front of the mart.

When Dori and Luke stepped out, I leaned over and pushed the passenger door open. As Dori grabbed the outside handle, I said, "Hurry, get in, now!" And then I went back to repeating the license number.

Before they were settled, I took off, watching Samuel's buddy walk back to the sedan in my rearview mirror.

"Get your purse out! Write this down!"

When she was ready, I told her the number, and finally said, "Samuel Vaullie. He was in that car!"

"Which car?" Dori turned to look out the back window.

"The sedan. Get my phone out of my purse and call Patrick Crane right now! His number is on a piece of paper in the front pocket. Tell him where we are and that we spotted Samuel."

Patrick picked up right away. Dori put him on speaker, explained what was going on, and read him the license number.

"Are they following you?"

"No. No one's behind us." The road behind me was black.

"Good. Keep a sharp eye, though. I'll send out an alert, but they're probably already tucked away in the hills somewhere."

"Yeah. But Samuel's here. The idiot! And, now you can hunt down his ass!" Dori said.

"Right." Patrick sounded a little less optimistic than Dori. "I need to get on this, but I'm going to want a description of the other men. Call me when you get back."

"Sure." We signed off.

"Did you notice a skinny sandy-haired guy when you were in the mart? Could you identify him?" I asked Dori. "I only saw him from the back, and the guy in the passenger seat was in shadow."

"I saw him," Luke spoke up. "I saw him."

"Good. Why don't you describe him to Dori, and she can write it down."

"Yeah, I can do that." He leaned forward in his seat. "We're going to get their asses!"

"We sure are, Luke!"

While saying goodbye to Dori and Luke in front of their former neighbor's home, we agreed they'd be the ones to call Patrick with the description of the men with Samuel. After that, I headed straight to the motorhome. It felt like it'd been four days since I left Cal's yard, when it had just been that morning. I was so happy to see my pets and my pint-sized bedroom that I sprawled out on the bed next to Alice and was out before I bothered to remove my clothes or brush my teeth.

Walking across the yard the next morning to where I left the hatchback, I came upon Cal squatted down at the back of the car, fingering the area around the missing taillight.

"How'd you manage this one?" He looked at me over his shoulder.

"The short answer is it was shot out by a guy who was chasing us down."

"Now that's one I ain't ever heard before, but comin' from you I can't say I'm surprised."

"What do you mean by that?" I put my fists on my waist.

"Well you do get yourself into some nasty fixes, woman."

"It's not like I go looking for trouble."

"Maybe not, but it sure has a way of finding *you*." He stood up and nodded toward the front of the car. "And the dent? How'd you come by that?"

"I ran into a small boulder." I held my hands up to demonstrate the size of the rock.

"Got a problem with your eyes?"

"No," I said, defensively. "I didn't see it behind the bush."

"I won't ask what you was doin' drivin' over a bush."

"Like I said..." My voice was taking on that impatient tone that always seemed to creep in when I was talking to Cal, so I forcibly dropped it a note or two, and continued. "I was trying to avoid being killed."

"Looks like you managed it." He took his cap off, looked me up and down and wiped his forehead with his sleeve.

"Yeah, I did," I said, thinking Cal was one unique man, and not exactly the type I ever thought I'd have to rely on. Yet there I was, once again, apologizing and asking for his help. "I'm sorry about the car. I'll pay for the repairs. Also, I apologize, but I'm going to need to stay here a night or two longer, until I can find another place to park the motorhome."

"Nobody's askin' you to leave. You can stay as long as you like."

"Thanks. Just let me know the cost of the repairs." I started to walk back to the motorhome.

"I'll only charge you for the parts. We'll call it my gunshot discount."

"What?" I turned to look back at him.

Slapping his cap against his thigh, he set it back on his head and pulled the brim down low over his eyes. They were just visible enough for me to see that they were smiling.

Smiling back, I walked away. I had to admit it. Cal was growing on me.

When I reached the motorhome, I called V.A. to let her know I was back, and to ask about using the shower. She told me she didn't have patients that afternoon, so I could come anytime after one.

I decided to eat my lunch at Dusty's, because I hadn't had any time to fill my little fridge—not that there would have been anything of interest other than almond butter and yogurt.

As I entered the restaurant, I saw Patrick Crane on his usual stool, with Dori behind the counter and Luke bussing a table, like they'd never left. Dusty handed plates through the pass-through to Dori, and exchanged a few words with Patrick before disappearing into the kitchen.

While walking over to take the stool next to Patrick's, I became conscious that my pace had slowed, my shoulders had relaxed, and I had let out a deep breath—as if I passed through the gates of home. Wow. I turned around to stare out the windows at the trucks parked in front of the diner and the smattering of buildings across the street that were two coats shy of an actual paint job. How that could be? How could a city girl feel more at home in this dry spot on the map than in L.A. or New York? And am I willing to stay long enough to find out?

CHAPTER TWENTY

At my most contrite, I asked Cal if I could borrow the hatchback for my dinner with Noah, and was thankful when he was fine with it. He didn't even bring up the subject of my mishaps in L.A., other than to say it was going to be a while before he'd be able to make the repairs. I wasn't too worried about the missing taillight. In Harmony I was more likely to share the road with coyotes than cars.

With the uncertainty regarding the length of time it was going to take before it was safe to show my face again in New York or L.A., I realized it was unfair to continue to rely on Cal's generosity. Shifting my left foot to try and find a little more room for it, I contemplated asking Cal about renting the little car. It wasn't exactly a great fit for me, literally, but it would be cheap, and with my current budget, cheap was good.

As I approached Noah's ranch, hearing the gravel crunch beneath the tires, it was with anticipation and trepidation. There was no denying Noah awakened my inner Eros. That first flush of mutual attraction is a high like no other, impossible to ignore. I was able to repress it some while in

New York, but when encircled once again within the intensity of Noah's own desire, the walls of resistance tumbled.

I was old enough and experienced enough to know that Eros is a god that built his kingdom on a foundation of sand. But, it's a place with a powerful pull, where for a few fleeting moments the rest of the world fades to black while you dance to music only the two of you can hear.

The question was, with Noah, what would be left when the inescapable tide washed that kingdom away and everyday life flowed in? He was a self-reliant rancher, seemingly content to spend the rest of his life among the red rocks and unpretentious people, and I was, what?

I still didn't know the answer to that one. As I looked through the front windshield at the sharp peaks silhouetted in the distance, however, I felt like I was getting closer.

I related the abbreviated version of the events of the past few weeks, including the previous day's incident in L.A., to Noah, over a yummy stew and cornbread. The guy really did know his way around a kitchen. When I finished, I leaned down to pet his dog Trudy, who was curled up at my feet, and waited for his censure.

It didn't come.

Picking up his wineglass, he scooted his chair back from the table where he had been sitting opposite me, stretched out his long legs and crossed them at the ankles. "How's your head? You still feeling any side effects from the roughing up?" was the first thing he asked.

"No, I mean, not many, just a knot." I automatically reached up and felt the lump under my hairline. "And a few bruises. They're healing, though."

"Concussions are nothing to fool with."

"They said it was mild, so I should be fine."

"Good." He nodded his head, then asked, "Criminal activity aside, how'd you like New York?"

"Manhattan is great. It's exhilarating to share the sidewalks with people energized by their work and the culture. Everyone operates at all-out mode in that city–from the restaurants to theatres, to the museums and Central Park–it has so much to offer."

"Sounds like you kept yourself busy."

"No." I shrugged. "Mostly I sat in my cousin's basement apartment in the Bronx and stared at feet."

"Feet?" He stopped his glass halfway to his lips and smiled.

"Yeah." I smiled back. "Anything you want to know about them, I'm your girl."

"I'll keep that in mind. So, not *everyone* in New York is in all-out mode."

"I guess not. But then, I wasn't there very long."

"You plan to go back?"

Hesitating, I fingered the corner of the placemat. "I don't know," was the best I could come up with. "My boss at the publishing company is allowing me to telecommute, so I don't really have to get back there for work. And, I'm not supposed to return until law enforcement has broken up the trafficking ring anyway."

"You're never going to live there again." He reached out and set his glass on the table.

"Oh, really?"

"It's in your voice. If you have to work that hard to drum up enthusiasm for the idea, why would you give it a second thought?"

"Good question. Maybe I didn't allow it enough of a chance. Maybe spending my entire life in one spot made it that much harder to feel comfortable in a new place."

"No. It's not that."

"You sound so sure of yourself."

"I am. And so are you. You know exactly where you *do* and *do not* belong. You just can't shut off the doubt in your own brain long enough to hear it."

"So, what? Did you make a pilgrimage to guru-land while I was away to discover the meaning of life?"

His eyes smiled. "My guru was my grandfather. He taught me that the truest voice I'd ever hear was the one coming from my own gut. Smart man." Noah slid his legs back under him, stood up and walked around to my side of the table. Clicking his tongue, he gestured to Trudy, who trotted to her bed by the stove, curled up and rested her head on her paws.

How'd he do that? If I clicked my tongue at Mr. B, he'd probably just turn his bloodshot eyes up at me, wondering what in the heck I was doing.

"Scoot over," Noah made a brushing motion with the back of his hand.

After I scooted down the banquette, he moved in next to me, so that our thighs were just inches apart. Resting his right arm on top of the cushion behind my back, he held my eyes with his. "Check your own gut, right now, Syd. What's it telling you?"

Shit. Why were we doing this? "Okay, I'll play along." I took a deep breath. "You're right. New York wasn't for me. I wasn't happy there, and I don't think that was going to change no matter how long I stayed."

"Good. We're making progress."

"Thank you, oh great and wise Noah." I turned up the corner of my mouth.

"You're welcome. No charge."

"Gee, thanks."

"But, that's only half of it. Now that we've established you don't belong in New York..." Reaching his hand out and covering mine, he leaned in and asked softly, "Where do you want to be, Sydney?"

That isn't fair! I glanced over at him and caught the heat in his eyes. Of course there is nowhere else I want to be right now. Look at you. You're as sexy as all get-out and a good guy to boot.

"Sydney?" He kissed the hollow of my neck.

"Okay, here. I want to be here." I pulled my head away so I could keep my wits about me. "But, that's tonight. There's the little matter of the rest of my life."

"It's not just tonight, and it's not just here where you want to be." He kept his eyes on me. "It's in Harmony, and you know it."

"Harmony! That's nuts. I only ended up here because I took a wrong turn."

"Or, a right turn."

"Again, with the guru stuff." I frowned. "I've spent a total of what? Ten days in Harmony? Ten days isn't enough time to decide whether or not you want to make a long-term commitment to a place. And, I know you have deep roots here, but you *have seen* Main Street, right? There's nothing there. How would I make a living?"

"You just said you were going to telecommute."

"I know, but that's just temporary. I don't want to be a copy editor the rest of my life."

"But you do want to be a writer."

"Yeah." I tried to recall when I would have told him that. "Again, I know this is your home, but the potential for subject matter around here is pretty slim, unless I decide to start freelancing for *Outdoor Magazine*. I could always interview Cal about the top ten reasons to use coonhounds to hunt game."

"You wouldn't be imprisoned here, Sydney." He rubbed his calloused hand over the back of mine. "We do have a highway that runs through town, and an airport not too far off that'll take you anywhere in the world you want to go. "And don't you writers get your inspiration from in here anyway?" He kissed my temple. "If I remember my high school English class correctly," he pulled back, "Emily Dickinson hardly left the house."

"I don't do poetry, and I don't look good in white."

Letting go of my hand, he gently tugged my shoulder so I was facing him straight on. "We're just dancing around the main point, Sydney. Whether you want to admit it or not, Harmony has a hold of you. Why else of all the places you could have hidden out from your trafficking buddies did you choose this speck on the map?"

I started to say it was because it would be a lot harder for them to find me in this lost wedge of high desert, but he cut me off before I had the chance.

"No." He shook his head. "Whatever you were about to say was going to be a rationalization. Fact is, when you needed a place to go, this was the first place you thought of, because you wanted to come back. You want to be here. You just can't allow yourself to believe it."

"No, I can't," I protested. "Because there's absolutely nothing about Harmony that was ever in my plan for my life. Not the sparse terrain, treeless mountains, or weathered buildings. Not men with multiple wives or mechanics with pronghorn heads in their ice chests. Not dentists who fill in as veterinarians or ranchers who read *The Scarlet Letter*." My eyes softened as I recalled that first conversation about his book club's choice of novel. This was one unique man. And, the most endearing thing was he cared enough about me to get me to cut through my own crap.

But, I had to give reality one more shot. "Again, though, Noah, how can I want to stay here?" I combed my hair back from my face with my fingers. "A place so unlike L.A., or any other place I've ever known? And, how can I have become connected to it in so little time? It's crazy."

"We're wired to sense right away whether to trust a place or a person. It's how we evolved. It doesn't take a lifetime. It doesn't even take ten days, if you're paying attention. Dorothy didn't stay home after she returned from Oz, you know."

"No. I didn't know."

"She went back there."

"She did?"

"Oh yeah, there was a whole lot more to her life than one trip down the yellow brick road."

"How about that. Do the other ranchers around here know this side of you, by the way?" I smiled.

"I don't believe the subject of *The Wizard of Oz* comes up much on cattle drives." He smiled back then pulled me to him.

"I wouldn't think so," I said, right before he kissed me.

"Anything else you feel connected to?" He pulled back, slid off the cushion, stood up and held his hand out to me.

"Yes," I said, caught up in the crystal blue of his eyes.

"Good." He held his hand out, and when I put mine in it, he helped me to my feet. "You know, in case you ever need someone to help you find Zion Park."

"I can find Zion Park." I frowned at him as I tugged on the back of my sweater with my free hand. "I made it all the way here from New York without getting lost once."

"Good to hear." Wrapping his arm around my shoulder, and guiding me through the kitchen, he kissed my neck and whispered in my ear, "But now, it's time to check out those bruises."

"And check them out, he did–thoroughly.

Afterward, lying pressed to his side, I felt his chest rise and fall in a slow and steady rhythm.

It was the most comfortable I'd ever felt in someone's arms. I snuggled in closer. Was I home?

Grab your copy of Book 3 in the Sydney Roberts Series

& Let the adventure continue!

Back in Harmony, Utah, Sydney Roberts has slipped out of her business pumps and into snowshoes and trouble. Sinister Samuel Vaullie is still lurking out there, his demonic streak growing wider by the day. This time Sydney's determined to stop him—no matter how far or dangerous the pursuit. She's also determined to come to terms with why she would boomerang right back to the parched and dusty one-horse town of Harmony—a town whose idea of culture is round dances and branding parties. Did she miss Cal? V.A.? Buffalo Bolognese? Really? Or was it Noah—a man whose lure was as hot as his branding iron and whose character was as strong as the metal from which it was forged?

www.ingramcontent.com/pod-product-compliance
Lightning Source LLC
Chambersburg PA
CBHW020610180626
46810CB00007B/2715